Kay Kinnear

© Kay Kinnear 2006
First published 2006
ISBN 1 84427 165 X
ISBN-13 9781844271658

Scripture Union, 207–209 Queensway, Bletchley, Milton Keynes, MK2 3EB,
United Kingdom
Email: info@scriptureunion.org.uk
Website: www.scriptureunion.org.uk

Scripture Union Australia, Locked Bag 2, Central Coast Business Centre,
NSW 2252, Australia
Website: www.scriptureunion.org.au

Scripture Union USA, PO Box 987, Valley Forge, PA 19482, USA
Website: www.scriptureunion.org

The right of Kay Kinnear to be identified as the author of this work has been
asserted by her in accordance with the Copyright, Designs and Patents Act
1988.

British Library Cataloguing-in-Data
A catalogue record of this book is available from the British Library.

Printed and bound in Great Britain by Creative Print and Design (Wales),
Ebbw Vale

Cover design and illustration by PRE Design
Internal design and layout by Author & Publisher Services

⮑ Scripture Union is an international Christian charity working with
churches in more than 130 countries, providing resources to bring the good
news of Jesus Christ to children, young people and families and to encourage
them to develop spiritually through the Bible and prayer.

As well as our network of volunteers, staff and associates who run holidays,
church-based events and school Christian groups, we produce a wide range of
publications and support those who use our resources through training
programmes.

Leyla's country, Kryzkalkystan, is fictional but the troubles her family experienced are true of some countries in the world today. If you would like to know more about such problems and lack of freedom, you could log on to Amnesty International at www.amnesty.org or www.controlarms.org

For Arran Luca Marvin
who has brought us such joy.

Special thanks to readers Hayley Cox and Tilly Hankins, Hugh Myddelton School, London, and Xavi Maddison, Weston Park School, also in London.

Chapter 1

"GRAN, WHERE'S MY PE KIT?" That's me shouting.

"WHERE DID YOU LEAVE IT, CASSIE?" Gran shouts back.

Grown-ups say funny things. If I knew where I left it, would I be asking?

I pace round my room looking. It's a strange shape, my room, skinny and it turns left at the end. That's where my desk is. Heaps of stuff under it. Yeah, there's the PE bag.

I open the bag and reel back. Pfaah! What a pong! There's a damp towel in there since last week and everything smells like Wilbur when he's wet. Wilbur is Gran's awful old dog. He hates me and I hate him, but I don't tell Gran coz she loves him. Wilbur pretends to like me too when she's around. It's our secret.

I hold the kit as far from my nose as I can and go to find Gran in the kitchen.

She's at the counter making tea.

"What's that smell?" she cries and whirls round. She's wearing her Save the Whales blue T-shirt and jeans. She can't be working today.

I drop the stuff on the floor. I imagine wiggly stink lines coming out like they do in cartoons. "Could you write me a sick note for PE?"

"Are you sick?" Gran asks.

"No, but I can't wear that smelly kit, can I?"

"I'll write you a smelly kit note then. That's truthful," Gran says.

"Grannnnnnnn!" I wail. "Miss Short will go ballistic."

Gran rumples my hair. It's curly and short so people do that a lot. "I'll wash your kit and drop it off at lunchtime."

I hug Gran and say, "You're a star." And I listen to a small lecture about remembering to dump my kit in the laundry basket and this is the last time she'll bail me out and stuff like that.

I nod and smile, and she and I both know it won't be the last time for anything. She's great, my gran. She's always there for me. And she looks so cool. She wears spike-heel boots and a poncho and maroon nail varnish. She's got green eyes and very short, curly hair like me too, and we're both skinny beans so people think she's my mum.

Well, she's all the mum I've got, as it happens, coz my *real* mum is in heaven with God. My dad's at sea on his oil tanker and he comes home sometimes. But it's just Gran and me mostly.

I eat my fruit and muesli. My mate Georgia calls it hamster food, but I like it. I munch and wonder what to do about my next big problem. I've spent some of the school dinner money Gran gave me. Me, Georgia, and Tabs went down the shopping centre on Saturday. My Wednesday pocket money was long gone. So I borrowed a dinner's worth of cash and thought maybe I could do a job for extra money and put it back. Bath Wilbur or something disgusting like that. Only I forgot… till now.

Gran interrupts my thoughts. "I'll phone the dentist for a check-up for you. Sometime this week if he's got space. OK?"

"OK," I say and go back to my room. I look longingly at my money bank. Pasted on it is a notice:

SAVE! SAVE! SAVE! SCHOOL TRIP ONLY!!!

I gave Gran the key coz I know what I'm like. Wish I hadn't.

I walk to my school. We live at the edge of our city, so it's near the country, and there are lots of trees. It's nice. The school isn't far and too soon I have to hand in the dinner money envelope to the school secretary. I scamper away before she can count it but she catches me at the door.

"Cassie, come back! You're a day short!"

"Ummmm," I mutter, thinking madly. Then it comes to me. "Gran is making me a dentist appointment."

She says, "So you'll be away one lunchtime."

Grown-ups can be helpful if you give them a chance. I didn't lie, did I? I *might* go at lunchtime. It's always been after school before, but it could be different this time. I stand there, waiting, helpful, but not saying yes.

"Off you go, Cassie," she says, peering at me and wondering why I'm still there.

Tabs comes up behind me as I come out of the office and grabs my arm in an iron grip.

I yelp and cry, "Let go!"

Tabs is one giant girl and never knows her own strength. Then I remember how she brings her own lunch, with twice as many goodies as anyone else. Maybe I can beg a sandwich off her on Friday.

Problem solved and I'm happy. I can usually work things out. I'm a flexible kid. There's only a very little niggle at the back of my mind. About being not exactly honest. Niggles are so annoying.

Chapter 2

After lunch is PE. It's a stupid time to go bouncing about with pizza and salad and stodge pudding churning round inside. At least I've got clean kit to wear, no thanks to me.

Today Miss Short has lined up three relay teams to race across the gym. My mate Georgia is just across in the next line so I won't get away with scorching up to the end and back. I like to run but Georgia insists it's well sad. Georgia is little and pretty with a long blonde ponytail and big blue eyes, but she's got a razor tongue. She makes fun of people who try.

"Hey!" I say softly.

"See how slow you can run without Shorty noticing!" Georgia hisses back.

Miss Short is nearly two metres tall with legs that go up to her armpits and a face that would look better on a horse. Even Gran, who hardly ever speaks an unkind word, giggled that Miss Short didn't suit her name. Georgia, of course, was the one who started calling her Shorty, or Shorty Knicks. Now the whole class does – not to her face of course.

As usual, I've got a double problem. I've got to run slow enough to please Georgia, but fast enough so that my team won't hate me and Shorty start yelling at me for slacking. PE never used to be so stressful!

Well, I just about manage it. Except Ali behind me pokes me in the ribs after we lose the relay and says, "You blew it for us."

Tough.

Next, Shorty organises us into a robot line. She demonstrates a wicked robot, she's all angles and elbows anyway. Georgia and I get the giggles.

Georgia whispers, "Hope Shorty won't have us doing junk like this on the school trip. I intend to chill out, being away from Jasper and Hortensia."

Georgia calls her mum and dad by their names.

Me, I don't intend to chill – no way. I'm doing canoeing and abseiling and go-karting and great stuff like that, but I don't say so to Georgia. (And it all depends if I save the money and get to go!)

Georgia's group starts off the robot, raising their arms stiffly up and down. Tabs' group is pumping knees. My bunch is bending from the waist. Completely daft, but Shorty looks pleased – I bet she's thinking gangly robots are just her kind of people. After a while, she blows a whistle and we all add on one of the other moves. TWEET! And we do it again. It's so funny. Total chaos.

TWEET! again and PE is history.

At break, I drift over to the trees at the far end of the playground with Georgia and Tabs. We lean against the trunks, a safe distance from the boys' kick-around.

"It's less than ten weeks to the school trip!" Tabs whoops. (She keeps a countdown calendar.) She punches a tree branch for joy and breaks it. Like I said, she doesn't know her own strength. We hide the broken bit up among the leaves so some snoop doesn't report us for vandalising. Tabs looks red and sorry. Inside, that loud, strong girl is marshmallow.

Then she brightens. "My mum bought me a new backpack. It's brilliant. It's got all kinds of pockets and zips and places for sandwiches and stuff."

I slump against the tree. "Lucky you. I'll probably be stuck all alone in class with a clueless supply teacher."

"You *won't!*" Georgia disagrees. "Your gran's a pussycat – she'll cough up in the end if you don't get the money saved."

"Not this time," I moan. "She's dug in her high heels to teach me a lesson. She'll pay £10, but she says I've had plenty of time to save the other £40 from my pocket money."

I stare straight at Georgia. "I'm supposed to learn to stop buying junk I don't really want. Junk that *some* people I won't mention talk me into getting."

Georgia is retying her ponytail and takes no notice. "We'll send you a postcard," she says, smiling sweetly.

(POSTCARD)

To Cassie
Having a
mega-cool time.
Studying hard?
Poor you.
Love, Georgia
and Tabs.

Home

11

"Oh, Georgia, that's horrible," Tabs says and thumps me on the shoulder. I almost fall over. I think it was Tabs' idea of a comforting pat.

The bell rings and we amble back towards class, aiming to be the last to go in. But when we get there, Shorty has a surprise waiting for us.

Chapter 3

"Sit down, boys and girls. I want to introduce a new pupil," says Shorty.

Crash and scraping of chairs, and we drop down into our seats staring at the new girl with Shorty. She is small with very bright brown eyes and she looks scared. I'm surprised to see she's wearing a headscarf. Our school has Indian kids, Kurdish kids and a few Chinese but nobody wears a scarf in school. I've only seen them on TV.

Shorty says, "This is Leyla Rashid. Leyla comes from KKKK..." Shorty clears her throat and tries again, rasping out a name full of sharp sounds. She writes it on the board. KRYZKALKYSTAN. Shorty smiles at Ali and says, "Since that's your home country too, Ali, I'd like you to be a special friend to Leyla."

Ali scowls. He hasn't *told* anyone his "home" country. He always says he's British. Shorty informs us that Leyla's been here six months and we're all to welcome her. Not noticing Ali's face like thunder, Shorty shows Leyla to a seat next to him. Then we get on with history.

At break, I see Leyla standing alone in a corner so I stroll up and ask her if she speaks English.

"Ye-ss," she says slowly. "I go to another school before here. I learn."

"What's that on your head?" bawls out Kevin as he races by. I glare at him but he grins, showing the gaps where his front teeth used to be before he fell off his bike.

"*Hijab*," says Leyla.

"Oddjob?" asks Georgia, who comes to join us. She is smiling sweetly. I don't trust that smile. It means trouble.

"No, *hijab*." Leyla touches her pale blue scarf. "It is for religion. I am Muslim." Leyla speaks softly with space between the words.

I change the subject. "What town did you live in in KKK—". Nah, can't manage it.

"Kryzkalkystan," says Leyla. She gives a small smile and seems to study her worn-looking brown shoes. Suddenly she looks up and stands straighter. "My brother say not to tell our city. Kryzkalkystan is enough." She lifts her chin at Georgia as if to say, take *that*.

Georgia rolls her eyes at me but the bell rings before she can blurt out a smart line. Fancy being from a place nobody but you can pronounce. And you can't even mention your town.

Half an hour later, I'm chewing my pencil on a maths ratio when a note lands on my book.

Wr hscrf tom

It's got to be from Georgia. Texting has frazzled her brain. I'm surprised she doesn't do her homework in texting. I battle on with my last ratio and then I glance over at Georgia's table and shrug. She's been waiting for me. She taps her head and points at Leyla.

I peer at the note again and then I get it. Wear headscarf tomorrow.

I mouth "why" at her, but she just smiles *that* smile again.

After school, Georgia says to a little group including Lauren, Mia, Josh, Kevin and Tabs, "If some people can wear stuff on their heads to school, we all can. I'm wearing my blue pompom tomorrow."

Tabs and Lauren look doubtful. But Kevin, who lives in a backwards NY baseball cap, except at school, punches the air. Josh is always up for trouble and he agrees too. Mia says nothing as usual.

I say, "I don't want a silly old hat on in school. We'll look like losers. We'll *be* losers."

"Come on, Cassie. It'll wind up Shorty Knicks big time. Can't you just see it?" Georgia claps her hands. "Shorty will have to call in the head teacher. We'll say – if some people can wear scarves and hats, why can't everybody?"

Georgia is a born stirrer.

I say, "I don't know. I'll think about it."

Georgia presses but I don't say any more. Sometimes I think she's a complete fluff-head, the rest of the time I'm sure of it.

Later, at home, Gran dishes up tuna casserole for tea and that cheers me up a bit, coz I'm worried about tomorrow. "Where is Kryzkalkystan?" I ask, practically giving myself a sore throat. "It's a place."

"Where is *what*?" she answers. "Look it up in the atlas."

I grab a couple of biscuits and go to email Dad. He might know.

> FROM: Cassie
> DATE: 9 April 19:15
> TO: Dad
> SUBJECT: Where is Kryzkalzistan?
>
> Hi Dad,
> Got all my maths ratios right today. Think I can
> steer your ship soon? (Joke.) That takes
> knowing numbers, doesn't it?
> Got a brain-twister for you. There's a new girl
> at school called Leyla. She's from a country I
> tried to spell above. She won't say her town.
> She wears a headscarf she calls by a funny
> name.
> When will you be home next?
> Love, Cassie

Dad's on his laptop for once and answers straightaway. His time zone is two hours ahead.

> FROM: Dad
> DATE: 9 April 21:25
> TO: Cassie
> SUBJECT: Maths genius
>
> Hi Cassie,
> Congrats on the maths. We'll start navigation
> lessons as soon as I get home. We'll hire a
> dinghy. (No joke!) Should be back about
> September, Cass.
> Your country has too many "z"s and not
> enough "k"s. It's Kryzkalkystan. It's in the
> Middle East and there's been trouble there in

the last few years. Don't press her for information. If she's a refugee, she and her family may have had a bad time. Just be her friend.

Have to run, time for my watch.

God bless you, love, Dad

A bad time. Is that why Leyla is here?

Chapter 4

Next day, I'm trudging through the school gate thinking about Leyla and dreading the morning. Our school is a big red-brick building about a million years old, except for the new light-coloured wing stuck on it for computers. Our classroom overlooks playing fields, so that's nice.

I haven't worn a hat, but a knitted nightmare is crammed in my pocket in case I can't face Georgia. How wimpy is that! In front of me is Leyla in her blue thingy and I call out her name.

"Leyla, would you like to sit at our lunch table today?" I ask. I'm remembering Dad said to be her friend.

Her face lights up. Then, suddenly, the light goes out. "No. But thank you for asks me," she says. She looks down at those worn shoes.

That's it? She's got a better offer? I don't think so! Must be something else.

"All right," I shrug. "Maybe another day."

She smiles but doesn't say anything. At least she's in fashion today since all our gang, minus me, have covered heads. I've definitely decided the knit bit can stay in my jacket pocket.

Beep! I get a text. It's from Georgia.

```
Stupd U.
Whar ht?
```

I spin round and there she is grinning from ear to ear under a blue pompom. "What did you ask *her* for? We've got our lunch bunch. And where's your hat?"

"I *wanted* to ask her," I say. "She doesn't know anyone. It's no big deal." Georgia thinks she runs the lunch table. "And it's too hot in school for hats."

It is, too, but that isn't why I didn't wear one.

"Chicken."

"Yeah, cluck, cluck."

The bell rings and we line up. Up ahead I can see Kevin's NY cap and Josh in a cowboy hat. Big Tabs is sporting a flowery number and looks a total geek. Lauren and Mia wear caps. Georgia isn't speaking to me now.

We file in, Shorty up front, and take our jackets off in the cloakroom. She stands outside the door telling people to hurry up.

"Leave your hats with your jackets," Shorty says.

But, hey, they don't, and clump to their tables and sit down. I wait, wondering what's going to happen.

Shorty is red in the face. She doesn't notice much, but she's twigged this.

Georgia is smiling *that* smile and waiting for Shorty to tell them off. Georgia is going to say, ever so sweetly, "Isn't it a new school rule to wear hats and scarves?"

Then she'll stare pointedly at Leyla.

Suddenly the class door opens. It's the head, Mrs Kendall. She's got bright red hair and she's OK, but she stands no nonsense. She says, "Assembly will be late today, 11 o'clock. It's a film and it hasn't arrived yet." She glances round the room and smiles, but she beams a look at Georgia.

"Splendid!" she says. "I see lovely contributions for the hat stall at this month's car boot sale. I'll take them now for safe keeping." She holds out a hand. "Georgia, you first."

The class gulps and stares. Will Georgia give up her hat? Five seconds go by.

Nobody moves.

"GEORGIA!" says Mrs Kendall.

Georgia inches into standing position, doesn't look up and sweeps off the blue pompom. "Thank you, Georgia," says Mrs Kendall. Resistance crushed, Tabs, Lauren, Kevin, Josh and Mia stream up to hand over their gifts to the hat stall.

"Thank you, all," says Mrs Kendall and heads towards the door. Just before she leaves the room, she turns. "If any of you didn't check out your hat donations with your parents, ask your mum or dad to collect the hats from my office. I always welcome a chat with parents."

I want to laugh so much my chest hurts. Georgia is fuming, her face pulled tight; Tabs is cherry-coloured. The other ex-hat wearers are scowling at Georgia. I peer round at Leyla. She looks puzzled. I think, I *hope*, Leyla hasn't taken in that this was about her and her scarf.

Shorty starts the lesson. In comes the class helper for reading who sits at Ali and Leyla's table. And all of us get down to literacy.

At lunchtime, Kevin has a go at Georgia for the loss of his precious NY cap. "Get your mum to collect it," she says, pretending not to care.

"You're joking. My mum would go ballistic if she heard about your airhead idea."

Ever the big peacemaker, Tabs says, "Cheer up, Georgia. Losing my flower hat is the best thing to happen this week. Dad makes me wear it every Sunday to church." She pats her head thoughtfully. "I'm not sure it's my style."

We nod, choking back our giggles.

I go to get a glass of water and pass where Leyla is sitting, empty chairs on either side of her. She is eating a hard-boiled egg (yuck!) and has a half-eaten tomato on her plate. Is that all she's got? Why isn't she getting free school meals?

I've got to stick my nose in, haven't I? I drop down into a seat beside her. I say, "You know, the school will give you free lunches. Didn't they tell you that? They're not too bad, really."

"Yes, they tell. But my br—family say, I take lunch."

Leyla or somebody in Leyla's family is making life hard for her. I wonder why?

Chapter 5

After school, Georgia, who has ignored me all through classes, decides I'm her bezzie again. "What were you saying to Oddjob at lunchtime?" she asks.

We're on our way, along with Tabs, to the shopping centre, our favourite spot.

"Oddjob?" I ask. Then I remember. "If you mean Leyla, I was just being friendly."

"What for?"

I don't answer. Georgia doesn't like goody-goodies. Anyway, just then we turn the corner into the shopping centre. I stroll over to study a shop window. I'm broke, so I'm safe from spending on anything stupid.

Famous last words.

Georgia has always got stacks of cash. She decides on a blue crop top. It makes her eyes look even bluer. I tell her so and she flashes a big grin in my direction. Life is easier when I'm on the right side of Georgia. Tabs buys us all Slush Puppies and we slurp round the centre staring in the windows and larking about, having a great time.

There's an outside stall and music blares from it.

GROOVY DANCING BEARS

NOW ONLY £2.99

The cutest little fluffy bears are grooving to the beat. It's so sweet. Tabs cries, "Let's all buy a bear! We can each choose a different colour and they can be friends."

Georgia and I groan. Tabs can be so soppy.

Georgia picks up a blue bear and says, "He goes with my new crop top." This time I groan alone. You wouldn't believe we're going to secondary school in the autumn.

But the bears are good fun, I admit, dancing away. Georgia and Tabs pick their bears and hand over their cash to the bored teenager running the stall.

"Come on, Cassie. Choose your bear," urges Georgia.

"I *told* you, no money."

"I'll loan you the £2.99. See, not even three quid, hardly anything." Georgia's eyes are bright. "You can pay me back in the next couple of weeks."

"No and no, I'm saving for the school trip, you know that."

"Don't be a saddo." Georgia makes her body droop. "You'll go on the trip, there's plenty of time. You just *have* to have one of these bears. Come on!"

I give in. I choose an emerald green one. The bears stop grooving the minute we walk away from the stall's music. Inside I kick myself. I've let Georgia talk me into spending money on what I don't want and don't need – *again*. She's got a satisfied smirk on her face when she looks at me. She does it for control. I stuff the grinning green toy in my bag and decide to go early to wait for Gran.

Gran works part-time at Pots-A-Plenty. It's a ceramics gallery at the far end of the centre. I think the shop should be called Pots-A-Money coz the dishes and jugs are dead expensive. There's a cream spotty vase in the window right now that costs an arm and a leg.

I open the door and it goes "Ding!" Gran looks up.

"Hi, Gran," I call. She's at the back of the gallery sitting at a scratched ancient wooden desk doing the accounts. There's a grim old cabinet tucked out of sight where they make tea and coffee. You'd think a smart shop like this would have nicer furniture for the staff.

"Hi, Cassie," Gran calls back. "Do you want some tea? I'll be a while yet. I'm hunting for an invoice."

"No tea, thanks." I flop down on the smart black leather customer chair. Ceramics magazines sit in a rack beside it. Putting off starting my homework, I leaf through one of the magazines.

It's amazing what people pay for dishes, even just little things. There's a titchy bowl pictured here with really tacky clashing colours and it costs hundreds of pounds. Think of all the school trips I could fund with that! Chance would be a fine thing.

Suddenly there's a thud from the back. Gran has a drawer pulled all the way out. "Here it is!" she cries. "The invoice was down the side. Now we can go home."

For tea, Gran makes spaghetti and I chop up a salad and lay the table. We eat with not much talk. I'm mad at myself about the bear, and Gran is quiet too. Even Wilbur, who usually snuffles round our legs in a disgusting way when we eat, has collapsed in his basket. I consider saying to Gran that Wilbur is lying doggo (Dad says it means keeping quiet). Then I look at her worried face and don't say anything.

Chapter 6

I do my homework and open my diary. I don't remember to write in it much. But I feel like it tonight even though the day was not totally sparkling. But I cheer up when I remember the hat retreat this morning.

Dear Diary
Tuesday
Yay! Got a better mark in literacy than last week.
Hat wearing a no-no - so funny!
Invited new girl to be with us for lunch, but she didn't want to. Dad would say I should have sat with HER. Wasted money on junk. When will I learn to stand up to Georgia?

I stare at the page and promise myself to do better. I'll try to find out what's up with Leyla. And I'll ask Gran for jobs to earn money. I look at my money bank with the SAVE! SAVE! SAVE! pasted on it and give it a smack.

Gran calls, "Cassie, where are you?"

I follow her voice to the kitchen. She is kneeling by Wilbur's basket. His mouth is lolling open and he's panting in great loud huffs. Wilbur is some kind of cross-breed with rough brown and black hair and a head too big for his body. He's not pretty when he's well and now he looks awful.

"What's wrong with Wilbur?" I ask.

"I don't know. He wouldn't eat his tea tonight so I was a bit worried."

I kneel beside Gran. Wilbur is the greediest dog ever, so she's right to be worried. He pongs even worse tonight than usual. I inch back from the basket.

"Let's try to get some water down him," says Gran.

I hold Wilbur's head and Gran pours spoonfuls of water on his hanging-out tongue. He seems to take it in and his huffs aren't quite so noisy. We look at each other, pleased.

Suddenly a great greeny-yellow stream gushes out of his mouth. It stinks something rotten. I run for newspaper and rags, and Gran grabs a bucket and mop.

I wipe up gunge while Gran scrubs off the basket and mops the floor clean. Together we lift Wilbur and put a different blanket under him.

We discuss whether we could get a vet to come out at night.

"He might be better in the morning," I suggest.

We turn to look at him and he has dropped off to sleep, snoring like a traction engine, but then he always does that.

"Maybe he just ate something nasty outside and now that he's rid of it, he'll be all right." Gran has such a hopeful sound to her voice that I nod.

We watch telly for an hour, with Gran hopping up every 15 minutes to check on Wilbur. He's sleeping

OK so we relax. I said before that Wilbur is a horrible old dog even when he's well. But Gran loves him so much that I try to overlook his faults. He pretends about me too. Wilbur kept Gran company after Grandpa died, before I came to live here.

Until two years ago, Dad and I used to have a house in a tiny village about 50 miles away. The village was called Little Sneesing – isn't that a fantastic name! Ah-choo, ah-choo! (We called it Sneezers.) But then he got this job on a ship and Gran was alone (apart from Wilbur) so I came to live here. There's so much more to do in a city. There's the shopping centre, cinema, sports matches, youth club at church… there was none of that in our village, so it works out well. I miss Dad though. Emails are good, but not as good as being with him.

It's bedtime and I kiss Gran goodnight and go to my room. Now's my time for praying. Dad says praying is like talking to God so I don't do the down-on-your-knees bit. I just walk round my room, taking off my clothes and pulling on my super-long T-shirt (pyjamas are so last week!). And while I'm doing that, I tell God about my day. I tell him what went wrong and then I feel we kind of plan together how I can do better.

As I clean my teeth, I'm thinking tonight's different, with more serious worries. Gran's pretending to be calm, but she's really stressed about Wilbur. I can't bring myself to pray for Wilbur; anyway maybe it's not right to pray for a dog. I'll email Dad about that. So I ask God to let Gran be happy again instead.

Then I get into bed and turn out the light. In the darkness, Leyla and her oddjob jump into my mind (I must ask her the right word again). I try to think how I can be her friend without annoying Georgia. Then I remember I'm a flexible kid. I can do both. And I thank God and go to sleep.

Chapter 7

Shorty perches on her beat-up old desk in front of the class, drops her pencil, does a complete jack-knife down to the floor to get it and starts taking the register. Tabs and Georgia, hatless I'm glad to see, are whispering and staring at Leyla. Luckily, her eyes are down reading her book. She bites her lip and wrinkles her forehead, studying the page. I see her point to the book and turn to Ali. He shrugs and looks away. Some help he is! Maybe he doesn't know the word either and hates to admit it.

Register done, Shorty says, "I want to collect now for the famine relief fund. You took home leaflets at the end of last week. Kevin, you can pass round the collection bucket." Kevin stands up and swaggers to the front. Shorty continues, "Those with envelopes or cash, raise your hand and he will bring the bucket to you. *Please*, do not get out of your seats. *Quiet, please*."

Leyla looks puzzled. She might not know the words – famine and relief. Most of the kids raise their hands. Not me! I forgot to ask Gran for money. And would I have two ps to rub together by this time in the week? Course not. Tonight is pocket money night. I'll ask Shorty later if I can bring mine in tomorrow. Georgia throws her envelope in. It makes a soft landing, letting everyone know there are notes inside and not coins. Tabs' envelope drops with a heavy clunk. Kevin passes the bucket round the class and then we try to learn where South America is.

On the way to lunch, I shuffle along slowly so I'll be at the back where Leyla always is. It's like she doesn't want to go to the hall. She is carrying a small plastic bag, her little lunch. I try again.

"Leyla," I say. "It must be a drag eating by yourself. Why don't you come and join us?" An idea strikes me. "I'll keep Georgia under control." Try anyway.

"That is, uh, nice, Cassie." Hey, here's progress. It's the first time she's used my name. "Thank you. But I cannot," she adds.

Why not? But I don't say it. I'll have to tell Dad it's very hard to be her friend. Is it worth the effort? Then I look at her face and she looks, yeah, like she *wishes* she could.

In the middle of the afternoon, the class gets a surprise. Shorty decides to try us on something weird called algebra. Shorty loves maths and is always pushing out the boundaries. I'm sure it's not in the looming SATS.

She writes numbers and *letters* on the board. What are they doing in maths? She explains and says x stands for 6 in this equation. The class, me included, looks blank. She writes another problem. "Now who can see what x is?" It was 6 only a minute ago. Why is it different?

From the back of the room, a quiet voice says "x is 4". The class goggles round. It's Leyla. Shorty absolutely beams and puts up another letters and numbers problem. Leyla answers right away, not even figuring with her pencil. Our very own maths genius! Ali is scowling. Some Kryz-whatzit mate he is. Next I

31

glance at Georgia, whose little face is scrunched tight. She's hopeless at number stuff, unless it's buying something. She won't be pleased Leyla's a whiz.

At the end of the day Shorty, passes out more paperwork. It's another leaflet and letter. I wonder how many trees are cut down for this school's messages home. Loads never make it out of our school bags. The rest end up as paper aeroplanes. This one is important though. It tells about the car boot sale to raise funds for furnishing the new computer wing and for our school trip. The way it works for the trip is like this: there's both a school fundraiser and some charity or business to pay part for each kid. And the kid and her Gran, or whoever, have to stump up the rest – this year, £50.

I walk home; Gran's not working today. I go in the door with the car boot sale leaflet in my hand to show her. I find her in the kitchen, crouched down beside Wilbur's basket.

"I took him to the vet," Gran says, "and she thinks it's an infection. I gave him his first antibiotic pill four hours ago." She glances up. "Don't you think he looks better?"

"He's not panting like last night," I say carefully. But his eyes aren't bright. When Gran gets up to give him fresh water, I touch his nose. It's warm. Aren't healthy dogs' noses supposed to be cold? Dad told me that. But I don't mention it.

Before going to bed I email Dad.

FROM: Cassie
DATE: 11 April 20:17
TO: Dad
SUBJECT: Wilbur and other stuff

Hi Dad,
Gran is worried. Last night Wilbur threw up all
over his basket and the floor.
The vet says he's got an infection. Didn't you
tell me a dog's nose should be cold? Wilbur's is
warm, almost hot. Do you think he'll be all
right? I was wondering whether it's OK to pray
for a dog? Do animals have a heaven?
Leyla, the new girl I told you about, turns out
to be a maths genius. I've asked her twice to sit
at our lunch table, but she won't. She doesn't
want any friends.
Hoping to hear from you soon.
Love, Cassie

Chapter 8

Whoah! What's wrong with Shorty this morning? She's got a face like a black cloud and she calls out the register through clenched teeth.

"ATTENTION, BOYS AND GIRLS!" She stands close to the front of the tables, sort of looming over us. She says, "I put the famine relief money collected yesterday in a brown envelope and put it in my desk. And I regret to report that it has *disappeared.*"

The class gasps. Disappeared! How?

"I waited till today to turn in the money because some of you," she glances at me, "forgot your donations yesterday." I slide lower in my seat. "The room was locked last night so the money was taken during the day."

She fastens her cold eyes on each of us, one by one. We follow her eyes too, seeing if we can pick out who's looking guilty.

I raise my hand. "Maybe a stranger came in at lunchtime," I say.

She shakes her head. "I ate lunch *here* yesterday." She bangs her old desk with her fist. "And I locked the room when I went out for a coffee."

Tabs and Georgia are whispering. I see them stare at Leyla. What do they know?

Finally we start lessons. Shorty is totally hacked off and no answer any of us gives is right. It feels like a week goes by before the bell rings for lunch.

It's a bad-food day too, some kind of yucky fish stew. And the veggie choice looks like what Wilbur threw up. I shiver thinking about it. I take salad, bread, yogurt and apple juice and go to our table.

"You know who pinched the dosh, don't you?" Georgia says. "Right, Tabs? Right, Lauren? Right, Mia?"

They nod but don't say anything.

"Oddjob, of course. Who else? Has anything ever been stolen out of our class before?" Georgia answers her own question. "No," she says. "And who is the only new person? It's got to be her. Leyla Oddjob."

"Leyla Oddjob," echoes Tabs.

"Yeah," say Lauren and Mia.

"We-ll," I hesitate. "That's not exactly proof." I picture her worn shoes and her little lunches. Maybe Georgia is right. We all look over to where Leyla sits alone, reading a book and eating an egg. No sign of a big lunch bought with stolen money.

And I make up my mind.

"I don't know where the money went," I say, plonking down my apple juice so hard it slops, "but I'm sure it's not Leyla."

Georgia makes her voice high-pitched and sing-song, "You're sure it's not Leyla! You know everything, you."

"You just like to give Leyla a hard time coz she's good at maths."

"Don't be a creep!" Georgia sweeps up her half-finished lunch and marches out of the hall. Lauren, Tabs and Mia glance at each other. Three little mice. Correction – two little mice and one big one. Tabs stuffs part of her lunch in her pocket. Then they follow Georgia.

That's me, pond life.

None of our lunch bunch looks my way in the afternoon. Like the money, it looks like I've disappeared too. Was I right about Leyla? Is it worth it? I wish Dad hadn't said to be her friend. Leyla doesn't want me as a friend, so why should I stand up for her and lose my own friends?

At the last bell, my former mates rush out of the room so I can't possibly talk to them or go anywhere with them. I stand with my homework book looking at Shorty. She seems really sad. She sighs and drops down at her desk. "Is there something you want, Cassie?" she asks, saying it like she hopes not.

"I've got my famine relief money to give you," I say. It's now the only money there'll be. Shorty sighs again.

Then I'm staring at her desk and I get an idea. "Could I help you search your desk for the lost money?"

"Whatever for?"

"Please."

Shorty drags open the top drawer and says, "The envelope was right here on top. See, it's gone." She sounds cross.

I'm shocked at the mess. Pencils, crumpled-up paper, rubbers, bulldog clips, pens, half a banana, an apple core, box of aspirin, Kleenex, and two South American maps from yesterday all crammed in the drawer.

"Could we pull the drawer all the way out?" I ask.

Shorty gives it a yank and almost drops the drawer on the floor. I panic. What if I'm wrong? Shorty will eat me for dinner. I shiver as we stare in together at the hole left by the drawer. Then I whoop for joy. Caught down the side is a brown envelope! I reach for it, smiling. The envelope rattles. I put my money in and hand Shorty the envelope.

"Cassie, you're a miracle!" cries Miss Short, hugging the envelope to her flat chest. "How did you know?"

"My Gran's desk at her work is just like yours and she's always losing stuff down the side. The drawers don't fit tight." I'm so chuffed the words rush out. "Just the other night I had to wait for her because she'd lost an invoice that way."

Shorty beams down at me and pats my shoulder. "Thank you so much, Cassie. I'll just go now and hand the money in at the office."

"Bye, Miss Short," I say. When I get outside the school, I text Georgia and Tabs.

> U Rong abt Lla
> ££ in dsk. C

I grin all the way home. I'm a miracle – Shorty said so. I'm also right about Leyla. And I send a little thank you towards heaven.

Chapter 9

Next morning I get up early and turn on the PC. There's an email from Dad.

> FROM: Dad
> DATE: 13 April 07:04
> TO: Cassie
> SUBJECT: Wilbur
>
> Hi Cassie,
> You can always talk to God about anything, even Wilbur. Pray for him if you want, but praying to comfort Gran might be better. You're a good kid, Cassie, to be concerned about Wilbur when we've agreed he's a horrible old dog. A hot nose doesn't sound good.
> Re: Leyla. *Everybody* wants friends. Keep trying. Maybe she's just very shy. Why not Google Kryzkalkystan and see what you can find out.
> Love you, Dad

I turn off the PC and pad barefoot into the kitchen. Gran is down on the floor again, spooning medicine into Wilbur. I make a cheese roll and choose a tomato and slip them into a plastic bag. Today's the day I haven't paid for lunch. But Gran's too worried about Wilbur to notice.

"Cassie, don't forget your dental appointment after school," she says. "I'll meet you there, OK?"

"OK, Gran. Hope Wilbur will soon be better."

"Me too," says Gran.

I set off early to school. I'm really looking forward to told-you-so-ing Georgia and the rest. I text Georgia.

U sory sspek Lla?
Shud be. C

Georgia doesn't text back. Weird – she's normally got a trigger thumb. Then I see Georgia and Tabs just ahead, strolling in through the school gate. Georgia never hurries.

I call out. "Hey, texting thumb broken?"

Georgia says to Tabs, "Did you hear something?"

Tabs hesitates. Then she shakes her head. "I didn't hear anything."

So that's it. My punishment for being right is to be invisible. My spirits bungee-jump to my toes and I stop dead. Leyla runs bang into me.

"Oh, so sorry," she says and giggles a little. It's the first time I've seen her lighten up. "I was daysleeping."

Then I laugh too. "I think you mean day*dreaming*."

"Oh yes. My bad English," she sighs.

"No, no. It's good. English is your second language, after all."

"No, English is my *third* language. I speak Turkish too."

"Mega-brainbox!" I cry.

Leyla goes pink and shakes her head. "We stay in Turkey on the way here from Kryzkalkystan." Then she claps her hand to her mouth, her eyes frightened.

What has she said that's so scary? I walk with her into school, me babbling away, but she doesn't talk again. Still, that's our best chat so far.

Shorty announces the discovery of the money and thanks me again in front of the class. I glance at Georgia, but she ignores me, staring up at the ceiling. At break, she, Tabs, Lauren and Mia whip headscarves out of their jacket pockets and tie them on. Then, with big grins, they parade back and forth past Leyla who is watching the boys play football.

Georgia says loudly, "You got any oddjobs to do tonight, Tabs?"

Tabs bawls back, "No oddjobs for me. How about you?"

Georgia spouts, "No, I wouldn't want any oddjobs either."

All four of them cry, "NO ODDJOBS!"

Well, that is nasty, big time! Leyla has taken it in too. How could she not? Head down, holding on to her headscarf, she walks away to the other side of the playground.

Just then a football hits Georgia on the back. Serves her right, I think. And the bell rings.

At lunch, I eat my cheese roll sitting with kids from the other Year-6 class. My ex-mates clearly don't want me. Georgia can be so much fun, but I'm beginning to wonder if I *really* want to hang around with her anyway. Gemma from the other class shares her cake with me, so life's not all bad.

After school, I head off for the dentist who is at the near end of the shopping centre.

On the way, I see Leyla up ahead meet a tall, dark-haired boy. He can only be about 19, but he's got a black beard and moustache. He scowls at Leyla and pulls her scarf further forward so you can hardly see her face. He leans down and is clearly telling her off about something. I suppose he must be a relative – her brother maybe? Poor Leyla, she gets stick at school and then from her family too.

The dentist says my chompers are tickety-boo. I guess that means good because we don't stay long. We hurry home, me to Google Kryz-thingy and Gran to check on Wilbur.

Web Images Groups News more
GOOGLE Kryzkalkystan
Search: the web pages from the UK
Car bomb rocks city; 100 casualties;
independent democrat (Inde) party suspected
...in the last two years, northern city Kizkul has seen numerous attacks. The military government has blamed them on the rebel independent movement infiltrating from the west. Others refute, suspecting government plants.
www.freerepublicKryzkalkystan.com/focus/f-news/17890/-16k
Cached – Similar pages

Refugees flee government clampdown on Inde party
...refugee flow from troubled Kryzkalkystan has tripled in the last two years. Families of Inde members have been targeted by the military

government. Reports of house arrest, false
imprisonment, and rumours of torture are
frequent.
www.refugeesfleeKryzkalkystan.com.tech-
report/275484/-28k
Cached – Similar pages

I read these and other pages. I can't understand most
of it, only it seems like the Kryzkalkystan government
is terrible. And they're putting in prison anyone who
protests – *plus their families*. I bet the protestors want
a country like ours where people are free. I wonder
about Leyla's family. Are they part of the people the
government is after? Did all of her family get away?
Why was she in Turkey? I wish Leyla would talk to
me.

Chapter 10

Saturday, no school!! Fabuloso! I lie in bed, stretching and wriggling my toes and looking forward to the day. Then I get up and put over two whole pounds in my SAVE! SAVE! SAVE! bank. Without Georgia talking me into buying junk, I've still got some of my pocket money. Maybe I can make the trip after all.

I decide to go to the library. That's free. Then swimming, where I've got a pass, so that's free too. My day is sorted. But then I walk into the kitchen and everything changes.

Gran is white-faced with red eyes. She tries to say something, but it doesn't come out. I look down at Wilbur's basket and I know he's dead. There's a blanket covering him and the basket.

Gran swallows and says, "I'm glad he's not suffering any more." She says it but she doesn't sound glad. She sounds very, very sad.

I go over and wrap her in a big hug. And she squeezes me back, like I'm the last thing she's got left in the world. Well, I am – apart from Dad, of course.

We should give him a proper burial, I say, to cheer her up. She brightens a little. "He could have a nameplate and flowers on his grave," she says. I agree, though I remember how Wilbur used to trample her flowerbed. I don't think he liked plants very much, but I don't mention it.

I get out my old wood-burning kit that used to be Dad's. Gran watches while I burn Wilbur's name in a piece of wood left over from when we got new floorboards.

WILBUR

It's hard to do curves with wood-burning. It's hard to write anything really, which is why I don't do it any more. Date of death would be nice, but after half an hour of scorching, just "Wilbur" will have to do.

"There's spare ground by the shed," Gran says. She looks at me. "Go and get dressed and let's get busy."

Once I'm ready, we carry Wilbur in his basket out to the back of the garden where he used to snuffle around. We take spades out of the shed and start to dig. He is a big dog, um, he *was* a big dog. The ground is hard and we dig away for what seems like hours. Finally the hole is big enough and we lay him in. Gran says a few last words about Wilbur being her faithful friend. Then, while Gran shovels earth over him, I pick yellow daffodils and get a jam jar to put them in. We set the flowers next to his nameplate.

Gran's eyes fill with tears and she says, "I bought Wilbur a beautiful new basket for his birthday next week." She gives one sob. "And now he'll never get to sleep in it."

There is nothing to say. I wonder if she'll take the basket back or whether she'll get a new dog. A puppy would be great! Then I feel guilty and glad she can't read my mind.

Gran makes sausages, mushrooms and crunchy toast for breakfast and then we go to the pictures. Gran wears her green and purple poncho and her best, really high, high-heeled boots. The poncho green makes her eyes look an even deeper green. Even when she's sad, she is one chic grandma, I think, not for the first time. I'm very pleased to look like her (except my eyes are brown). We don't mention Wilbur for at least two hours.

Later in the day, I email Dad the news.

FROM: Cassie
DATE: 14 April 16:37
TO: Dad
SUBJECT: Wilbur

Hello Dad,
Very sad news for Gran. Wilbur died during the night. We dug a grave and put a wood-burned nameplate I made and some daffs on his grave. Then we had cooked brekky and went to the cinema.
I Googled Kryzkalkystan and it sounds a terrible place. Lots of refugees running away.
Love, Cassie

Dad is on his laptop and answers an hour later.

FROM: Dad
DATE: 14 April 19:45
TO. Cassie
SUBJECT: Wilbur

Dearest Cassie,
You're a star for being so kind to Gran and helping her give Wilbur a proper send-off. She'll miss him very much. Be extra thoughtful for a while till she feels less sad.
Here's an epitaph (that's something written for

someone who's died) for Wilbur:

Wilbur, Ever Faithful Friend

Wilbur, ever faithful friend
Is never a dog to run away
Loyal to Gran to the very end
Barking, a dog to guard and stay
Until the time, alas, to record
Reliable Wilbur, gone to dog's reward.

Spur of the moment poem. If you think it's
good enough, print it out for Gran.
God bless, Dad

Chapter 11

Next morning, I reread Dad's poem and print it out with a fancy heading for Gran. She says it's lovely and pins it up on the kitchen notice board. I'm glad she doesn't cry again.

I put on my best gear (cargo trousers and a red stretchy-knit top) and we walk to church. We sing some songs – one of the ones I like most is "Amazing Grace". When I was little, I used to wonder who this Grace was and why she was so amazing. Then Dad told me it was about God's "grace" to us – the love he freely gives us – amazingly forgiving us when we do so much stuff that's bad.

Mr Dixon, our minister, is young and smiley and talks so you can understand, not like the OAP-type who used to be here. Dad once fell asleep and snored in one of his talks. Gran and I got the giggles and it was dead embarrassing.

The talk today is called "Christians going the extra mile for others". Mr Dixon points out that since God has given his only son Jesus to save *us*, then we should be more willing to help and be nice to *others*. He says, we shouldn't be put off when we aren't successful right away or we get rejected. At once I think of Leyla and I have this two-way conversation inside.

Me says that Leyla has said no to my attempts at friendship.

My niggle self says why didn't I sit down with her Friday at lunch?

Me says, well, she didn't want to join *our* table at lunch.

My niggle self points out that she didn't reject the idea of me sitting with her *somewhere else.*

Me says I didn't think of that at the time.

My niggle self asks why not?

Me admits that even though they're ignoring me, I'm still trying to keep in with Georgia and the rest and they don't like Leyla.

My niggle self says maybe I should find some better friends.

Me sighs and says but Georgia can be so much fun.

My niggle self wonders whether that fun is worth the rest of the hassle.

Me and my niggle self then get together and make a decision. I promise myself not to worry about Them and to keep on trying with Leyla. Reading a bit about her country, I think she could really use a friend. Then I remember Gemma from the other class and wonder if we might both join Leyla at lunch.

I start listening again to Mr Dixon who talks about new approaches and goes on to encourage just what I've been thinking. Afterwards we pray and I include Gran, Dad and Leyla in my thoughts.

My niggle self jumps in again (this gets annoying) and asks why I don't pray for Georgia?

Me says why should I?

My niggle self says maybe she needs help to be a better person.

Me thinks we'd need the whole church's prayers rocketing upwards to change Georgia. But Me gives in and does as instructed.

I have a little money to put in the offering bag this Sunday (even after part-paying off Georgia for the bear). Usually Gran coughs up some change for me. She smiles at me when she sees I've got my own coins. After the service Gran goes to Adult Bible Study and I trot along to Youth Group.

Over lunch, I tell Gran about the lunch money I spent on shopping. I tell her that I let the school secretary think something that wasn't true. I get going with honesty and don't stop till I reveal that I made a packed lunch while she was mega-worried about Wilbur.

Gran is so great. All she says is, "Thank you for telling me. But I won't expect you to use lunch money for other things ever again." I agree at once.

Nothing happens the rest of the day. I do maths homework, which I don't count as anything happening. We watch a movie on telly, not a doggy story, thank goodness, like *Lassie Come Home*, which was on last Sunday.

I open my diary, which I haven't written in much this week:

Dear Diary
Sunday
Decided to try again with Leyla.
You won't believe this, Diary, but I even prayed (a little) for Georgia, plus

confessed to Gran about lunch money.
Can you see my halo? Joke!

I'm looking forward to tomorrow. It feels like a new start. As it turns out, more of a new start than I am expecting.

Chapter 12

On my way to school, beep! I get a text from Georgia.

```
Lez B frnds.
G
```

I have to laugh. After all it's Georgia who's frozen me out. Maybe her thumb missed. She actually means "let's be fiends". She's strolling up ahead and turns round and waits for me. She acts like everything is normal. My sneaky suspicion is that Georgia hates one of her bunch slipping out of her control. Still, it's nice to be friends again. She presses me to go to the shopping centre after school, and after a while I give in.

The day goes by very dull. Late afternoon we're grinding through science – I wish instead we could go out and scoop up pond weed and fish for tadpoles, stuff like that. No chance. Leyla and Ali and two more kids have gone to the other class for special help.

Suddenly the school secretary appears at the door and calls Shorty over. They whisper for a minute and then Shorty asks me to go with the secretary.

"What's it about?" I ask as we turn towards the head's office.

"Mrs Kendall will tell you," she says.

Mrs Kendall looks up from a stack of papers and invites me to sit down.

"I've got unfortunate news for you, Cassie," she says.

What can it be?

"Your grandmother has had an accident."

My heart thumps. I see Gran lying in the road, her poncho a complete circle round her. I babble, "Is she, is she—" but I can't get the word out.

Mrs Kendall has jumped up and comes round the desk to take my hand.

"She's fine, really," says Mrs Kendall. "Your grandmother fell and broke her arm. She took a tumble outside Young's Pet Store taking back a dog basket."

Wilbur's birthday basket he never got to use.

"The heel broke on her boots and she slipped." Mrs Kendall is looking very sorry. "I believe she has also sprained her ankle."

I'm panicking. "Where's Gran now?" I yelp. "Is she in the hospital?"

"No, the hospital has set her arm in a cast and sent her home." Mrs Kendall smiles a really kind smile at me. "Your neighbour Mrs Barnes is outside now to take you home on her way to work."

Ten minutes later, I walk in the front door and call out, "Gran! Gran!"

Gran is lying on the lounge sofa, one foot propped up on cushions. Her right arm is in a sling.

I run and give her a hug. "Ouch!" she says. "Careful!" She adds, "I feel so stupid. I wasn't watching where I was going. My boot heel got caught in a crack in the pavement and broke." Gran laughs a little. "Serves me right for wearing such spindly spike heels."

I like her smart boots, but don't say anything.

"I'm going to need your help, Cassie." She hands me a notebook and pen.

"I've phoned Butterworths and ordered food and supplies, but they won't deliver till the day after tomorrow."

She dictates a little list for me to buy now, and I catch the bus to the supermarket.

I buy rolls and milk, cans of tuna, and stuff to make pasta for tonight. I stand in front of the melons wondering how to choose one that's ripe.

"Hello," says a voice. Here's a surprise. It's Leyla. "You leaves school today?" she asks.

I tell her about Gran and say I will be doing the cooking.

"I cook too," Leyla says, "for my family."

Then she shows me how to pick a ripe melon. You look for a smelly one. So we start sniffing away. Then we get the giggles, but we choose what I hope will be a good one.

I take the bus home. Gran sort of hops into the kitchen and tells me how to make tomato sauce for pasta. I chop an onion, squeeze a garlic clove, and fry them up in olive oil in a pan. I add some herbs from the store cupboard, and two cans of tomatoes and stir it round and cook for a bit. That seems to be it; this cooking lark is easy. I make a salad, which is what I do normally. I boil up funny tube-shaped pasta with a name I can't say. At least it's easier to eat than spaghetti. And we're ready.

We say thank you to God for the food, and then we tuck in. For pudding, we eat the melon, which is juicy and sweet, and Gran compliments me on my choice.

Then we make a meal plan:

Cassie's Meal Plan

Tuesday .... Tuna salad and the rest of the melon
Wednesday .... Grilled lamb chops, jacket potatoes,
.... peas. Fruit salad.
Thursday .... Baked chicken breasts, rice and salad.
.... Ice cream
Friday .... Pizza and salad. Ice cream
Saturday .... Fish'n'chips from the shop

Yay! Yay! I'm to get an extra £5 a week pocket money for my help till Gran is better. School trip in sight!

Chapter 13

Next morning, I get up early and email Dad about Gran's accident. Then I make our breakfast – tea and muesli and toast. Gran gives me a big kiss and says she'll be all right while I'm in school.

In the second subject of the day, Shorty is writing sentences on the board. I hear noises behind me. Kevin and Josh are pretending to spray Leyla's seat, making small shushing sounds. Leyla is at the side of the room reading with a helper. I catch Kevin's eye, and mouth out, "What are you doing?"

He mouths back something. It *can't* be what I think he's saying.

"What?" I mouth again.

"We're spraying for fleas."

Anger rushes up and nearly frazzles my brain. Who put them up to this? Neither of those losers could dream up such a skanky trick on his own. Then I look at Georgia. She smiles, shakes her ponytail, and gets up to sharpen her pencil. On the way, she pretend-sprays too. That is so horrible I feel sick. All the class sees and sniggers, except Leyla who is reading away quietly.

Shorty turns round and the disgusting business stops. But I don't stop feeling sick for Leyla. I notice Ali scowling, so for once he's on Leyla's side.

At break, I head towards Leyla. But she sees me coming, turns and walks to the far side of the playground. What's happened to my friendly melon shopper? Why the freeze? How many "extra miles", like Mr Dixon said, do I have to go? I glance over my shoulder and spot Georgia and Tabs smirking.

I spin round and march back to them. "Who started that rotten spraying trick?" I demand.

Georgia doesn't answer. Instead, she sing-songs, "I see your buddy Leyla can't wait to get away from you!" That's just what it looks like so I don't say anything and slump away.

After school, I make another trip to the supermarket for stuff Gran forgot on her order. I'm standing in front of the meat counter staring at lamb chops. They're so *small!* Have you ever noticed how titchy lamb chops are? It hasn't caught my attention before. I wonder which ones to buy, picking up one pack after another. A hand taps my arm. It's Leyla. "Look for more meat, not fat," she says and points to a pack at the back.

"Thanks, Leyla." I scoop up the pack, putting it in my basket. And I plunge in. "Why did you run away from me in the playground this morning?"

Leyla's face grows pink. "I am sorry. The class was doing horrible things. I am too angry to talk."

It's my turn to have a burning face. "I hoped you didn't see."

"Oh, I see. I ask Ali what they do."

"Leyla, I apologise for the class – so nasty – I don't know what to say." Then I change the subject and ask, "Are you in this shop every night?"

She laughs. She's got a nice bubbly laugh. "No, but often," she says. "My mother is ill so I shop and cook."

I think how I'd hate to shop and cook every day. I wonder if her mum is ill all the time or just ill for now like my gran. I don't like to ask. Instead I say, "Tell me again what your headscarf is called."

"*Hijab*," she says. And she spells it. "It tell people I am Muslim."

"Why don't Guler and the Kurdish girls in the other class wear a *hijab*?"

"Kurdish girls are Muslim, but they not wear *hijab*."

I ask, "Why is that?"

Leyla shrugs. "I don't know."

"What colour is your hair?" I blurt out the question. Then I'm embarrassed.

Leyla grins. "It is dark brown. If you are in my home, you see."

"So, you don't wear your – uh – *hijab* at home?"

She looks astonished. "Of course not!"

I say, "I'm a Christian, but I don't usually wear anything to show." I think about this. "I have a cross necklace I wear sometimes." I think about this some more. "I guess for Christians what you *do* is supposed to show who you are."

"Oh, yes," says Leyla. "What you do is very important for us too."

We leave the meat counter – Leyla hasn't got anything from there. Her basket has eggs in it, no mega-surprise. We go down the aisle to "Fruit". She picks some reduced price oranges and bananas, and I buy apples. Making chat, I say, "One day after school I saw you meet a tall boy. Is he your brother?"

She jumps and trembles a little. "Yes, he brother." I notice her English gets worse when she's flustered. "Brother say..." She stops and takes a deep breath. "*My* brother say I must not be friendly at school."

I'm shocked. How strange! I don't understand. Where's the danger in being friendly?

I start to ask. But she holds up her hand like a stop motion and shakes her head so I know not to say any more.

Chapter 14

Next day, I plan to meet Leyla walking into school. She doesn't know about my plan, but she always comes in at the same time. So I'm there to stroll in with her.

We stop for a minute and I ask her a question about maths homework.

Beep! It's a text from Georgia.

```
OK, C. Chuz.
Us or Oddjob.
G
```

Leyla sees my face. "Bad news?" she asks.

"Yes, in a way," I say, and jam my mobile into my pocket. Why should I have to chuz?

I spend some of class time doing what Leyla calls "daysleeping". I'm wondering how to act on Georgia's… um… ultimatum, I think that's the right word. Georgia and Tabs were my first mates when I moved here from Sneezers, my old village. They were so friendly and included me in their bunch with Lauren and Mia. Straightaway they invited me to birthday parties, stuff like that. It can be hard to be a new girl in a big school and they made fitting in really easy.

Then Shorty stops talking and we have a practice SATS test so I have to pay attention.

At lunchtime, having made no decision, I sit with Gemma again. Leyla, reading her book, eats, aargh, another hard-boiled egg. That girl will start to cluck soon.

The afternoon blurs by.

Today after school, I don't have to shop so I hurry home to help Gran.

She's on the phone, chatting away, with one leg stuck up in the air. She sees me and finishes her conversation.

"Hi Cassie." She scrubs at her head with her left hand. "My hair is driving me crazy. Can you help me wash it?"

"How will we keep your cast dry?"

We manage it with a big plastic bag tied over her arm. Then I blow-dry her curls and she hops out into the kitchen to supervise our tea.

Jacket spuds are dead simple in a microwave. Peas are, ho-ho, easy-peasy too. Gran, however, supervises the grilling of the titchy lamb chops. She hacks away one-handed at some apples to go with fruit cocktail for pud.

Over tea, I tell Gran about Georgia's text. She frowns and says, "Cassie, you shouldn't have to choose between friends. Surely Georgia and Tabs will come round in time. What's the matter with Georgia, anyway?"

I admit I don't know. Maybe she's jealous. "Georgia and Tabs were my first best mates here. We've had great times together."

Gran interrupts suddenly to say, "These are excellent lamb chops, Cassie. What a good shopper you are!"

I reveal Leyla's help and with the melon too. Gran is surprised, and I think again I should be able to have different kinds of friends. After all, I'm a flexible kid.

Chapter 15

I gathered up all my mates and hoped-to-be mates in my prayers last night. Maybe somehow it'll be all right today and I won't have to chuz.

So this morning, hating to do it, I take some pocket money (which should go into the Trip Fund) and set off for school. On my way, I pop into Patel's corner shop. I buy Tabs' favourite Chox Dropz and Georgia's Lemon Squeezers (so sour but she likes them). I hesitate and then also pull out the latest *Go Girl* magazine. I get 3p change. Hope this is going to work.

I'm right behind Georgia and Tabs as we go through the school gate.

"Hey," I call.

"Did you hear anything?" Georgia turns to Tabs.

"Nah," says Tabs.

I sprint round and stand arms-out in front of them. "Listen up," I say. "I've got a let's-be-friends peace offering for you both."

Tabs is interested but I can't tell about Georgia.

I hand over the sweets and the magazine. Tabs beams at me. She's not really my problem.

Georgia takes the Lemon Squeezers and turns the packet over slowly as if she'd never seen one before. Then she drops it on the path. She yanks the magazine out of Tabs' hands and it plops down on the ground too. Tabs has pocketed her Chox, I note.

Georgia stares at me. "So you think you can bribe us with sweeties? And a mag? Anyway, I've read that issue."

"I didn't know that," I mutter.

"You *would* know if you didn't hang around with riff-raff." Georgia sticks her nose in the air.

I straighten my shoulders and blurt out, "Why can't I be mates with you two *and* Leyla? After all, she needs—"

Georgia says, "I don't give a Turkey Twizzler what Oddjob needs. Cassie, you're either with us," Georgia taps her chest. "Or against us." She crosses her index fingers in the air. "Make your choice."

"Well, maybe—" says Tabs.

"Shut up," says Georgia.

I dither. "I'm thinking," I say. I want to talk to Dad. Why is he so far away?

Georgia stalks off. Over her shoulder she calls, "Lunchtime today for your answer. Otherwise you're out."

I pick up the magazine and lemon sweets and trudge into school. The class spends the morning "littering and numbing" as Georgia calls literacy and numeracy. I love reading and can't see why school makes it so boring. Numbers are not my best thing, although once in a while I get a flash of what it's about. But I'm not brilliant like Leyla. Anyway, for once I'm glad for numbo-jumbo – the problems are so hard I can't think about my troubles.

Lunchtime, I come slowly into the hall. Tabs and Georgia see me and wave me over. I try to smile, and can't. Shall I wimp out and sit with Gemma? I spot her in the far corner. I go to collect my food and I can't even decide what to eat.

"Come on, love," says the dinner lady, "you're holding up the queue."

Finally, I point to ham salad and take a mango yogurt and juice. I'm standing, holding my tray, and notice my yogurt carton jiggling. I'm *shaking*! Flippin' pancakes, what a saddo! I'm mad at myself and scrunch the tray against my chest to clamp it still. I march over and plonk myself down beside Leyla. A hard-boiled egg stops halfway to her mouth, she is so surprised. Then I'm glad. I've kind of made the decision, without really deciding, if that makes sense. (OK, it doesn't.)

"Hello, Cassie," she says, and smiles at me.

"Hi, Leyla." I look at her awful egg and think she'd like a change of food. "I've got too much ham," I say, starting to cut the slice. "Here, I'll give you some." I lift up half the ham.

Leyla shrinks back. "OHHH!" she shrieks. "NO! NO!"

I jump and my ham fork clatters down on my plate.

Seeing my open mouth, Leyla babbles, "Muslims not eat pork – pig not clean animal for us."

Whoah! I guess being mates with Leyla will be a bit tricky. "OK," I mumble. I pick up my fork and cut a bite of the dirty beast.

So far, it's not been a great day. I've wasted trip money on Tabs and Georgia and still I've lost my two bezzies. I've "chuzed" Leyla, whose ways I don't understand. I've "chuzed" a mate that, so far, I see only at school and the supermarket. Plus yesterday's practice SATS was the pits. I slump in my chair and shove my plate away.

Chapter 16

FROM: Cassie
DATE: 19 April 19:45
TO: Dad
SUBJECT: Sad

Dear Dad,
I had an awful day at school. My bezzies
chucked me out of their bunch. They made me
choose between them and Leyla, the girl *you*
said I should be friends with. I went to sit with
Leyla at lunch. All afternoon Georgia and Tabs
said horrid things about me in class. Well,
Georgia did. Tabs looked kinda nervous. On top
of all that, I did rubbish on yesterday's practice
SATS test.
Gran's ankle is better though. She's hobbling on
that foot now. She fixed tonight's chicken and I
overcooked the rice. Even my rice was wrong.
Love from your miserable Cassie

I wanted Dad to answer right away like he does
sometimes. But no. It wouldn't happen when
everything was bad today.

Next morning, the sun is shining and I feel better. At
least I've made my choice and don't have to puzzle
about it any more. Dad still hasn't answered but
maybe he will later. Also it's Friday, almost the
weekend.

At breakfast, I ask Gran if I can invite Leyla over
tomorrow. We could go swimming or just hang out.

"Where does Leyla live?" asks Gran and I admit I don't know.

"She uses the same supermarket so it can't be far away," I say.

More SATS stuff at school. I'm getting very fed up. I wish we'd just *take* the stupid tests and have done.

At break, I ask Leyla to go swimming tomorrow.

"I don't know to swim," she says.

"Didn't you have lessons at your school where you come from?" I ask.

"No swim pool for girls," she says.

I'm speechless. Do girls need different water from boys? But I don't ask – I don't like to bad-mouth her country.

"OK, no swimming." I ponder stuff to do. "We could listen to CDs at my house? Or play a board game?" (Bored games is what I call them.) "Or window shop at the shopping centre?"

"Thank you, Cassie," says Leyla. "But I must stay with Mama."

I leave it for the moment.

At lunchtime, I have another go. I sit with Leyla and try not to see the hard-boiled egg. It pongs eggy too. Today she also unpacks carrot strips and one of those bargain oranges. I've been careful not to choose ham or sausages. A cheese roll and salad should be A-OK.

I plunge in with my next idea to get together. "Leyla, if you need to stay with your mum, could I come over to your place?" I quickly add, "Just for a little while. I could bring her some flowers from our garden. Wouldn't she like that?"

I look at Leyla hopefully.

She bites her lip. I think she's going to say no, and she does. "I'm so sorry. My brother will not want you to come."

I nod. "I forgot about your brother."

I wish again that Dad was around – he got me into this Leyla friendship after all. I wonder what he would suggest. Then I know. He said it often enough. If at first you don't succeed, try, try again.

At afternoon break, Leyla and I watch the boys have a kick-around. When the ball is booted our way, Leyla surprises me with a swift, accurate kick straight back.

"Hey, you're pretty useful," I say. "You should have come to our school earlier. They'd have liked you on the girls' team. You should try out at Secondary School next term."

Leyla looks amazed and shakes her head. "My brother will not want it."

I'm getting sick of this interfering brother and I get another idea. "Is your brother home all day on Saturday?"

"No," Leyla says. "He w—" She stops and claps her hand over her mouth.

"What does he do, Leyla?"

She stands completely still for a moment. I wonder if she's deciding something. "I tell you and you can keep the secret?"

"Yes, of course."

"You sure?" Leyla's face is crinkled up. She's worried.

"Abso-blooming-lutely," I say.

Leyla takes a deep breath. Then she says very softly, "My brother works."

That's it? The big secret? Was her family some kind of royalty and nobody ever had a job before? I'm stunned. Finally, I ask, "What's wrong with that? Most grown-ups work."

"Cassie, you do not understand. We are asylum seekers. We cannot work. It is against the law. We get in trouble, you understand."

I don't understand. "If it's wrong, why does he work?"

"Because money we get is so small. Do not tell, please."

The bell rings. Other kids come near and we can't talk more.

Chapter 17

Dinner tonight is one of my favourites, pizza with four kinds of cheese, salad and toffee crunch ice cream. But I don't enjoy it much. I'm worrying about Leyla's family. Will they be sent away, back to Kryz-whatsit, if somebody, like a neighbour, tells on them? Or will they all be put in jail? I don't *think* this country jails 11-year-olds, but what about the others?

I'm thinking about *them* first of all; suddenly I think about me. Now that I know something that's wrong, should I tell someone? But I promised Leyla not to tell. Could they put *me* in jail for not telling what I know? My head starts to hurt.

"You're very quiet tonight, Cassie," Gran says. I'm washing dishes and she is perched on a stool drying them. "Have you worked out what to do about your friends?"

"Sort of," I mutter.

"You don't sound very positive."

Without meaning to, I give a big sigh. "I sat with Leyla at lunch. My old mates were pigs to me in the afternoon."

"Maybe those mates aren't worth having," Gran suggests.

"Maybe," I say, but I still feel bad. I want to tell Gran about the other thing, but I promised Leyla. I shouldn't have promised so easily, but I didn't realise it would be...

Gran interrupts my thoughts. "Let's play Scrabble when we finish the washing up." She's trying to cheer me up.

"Oh, Gran, thanks. But I already saw and heard too many words today."

"All right, love." Gran says and pats my shoulder.

Next morning, I shop again for Gran. She was going to phone in an order. But I ask if I can go to the supermarket because maybe I'll see Leyla. And I'll try to ask a few more questions. Like, why can't asylum finders – no, what is it, oh yes, asylum seekers – why can't they work and earn money? What has to happen before they can? I also wonder where her dad is. Maybe he died like my mum.

I look for Leyla at the reduced price stand. There are patched up boxes, dying lettuce and spotty bananas, but no Leyla. I go to the melon stand, no Leyla. I trolley round and round the supermarket after I've picked up what Gran wants, no Leyla. I catch the bus home and put away the grocery stuff and bring Gran a cuppa. She is practising walking round without limping.

"Go Gran!" I say. "You're doing great."

Gran gives me a big grin. "Now if I could just get rid of this!" She thumps her arm cast.

"Soon," I say. I pick up my homework book and notebook and say, "I might as well do my homework."

Gran raises her eyebrows. "On a *Saturday*?" She knows I always leave my homework to the last minute, like Sunday night.

"I've got nothing else to do. I'll *never* have anything else to do," I say. I realise I sound pitiful and try to smile. But I don't succeed.

"What's wrong, Cassie?" Gran sits down on the sofa and pats the cushion beside her.

I slump down next to her and say it's because I've lost my friends.

"But you have a new one," Gran says.

"But I can never hang out with Leyla – she always goes home. And she can't—" I stop. I'm getting too near telling Leyla's secret.

"What can't she do?" asks Gran.

"I can't tell you," I say. "I promised."

"Does that mean it's something wrong?"

"It's, oh, I don't know." Then I blurt it out. "She can't… she can't do anything with friends because her brother won't let her!"

Gran wrinkles her forehead. "Why not?"

"It's because… because he *works*," I say. "He's afraid, I think, maybe that somebody will find out and tell. It's something about being asylum seekers."

"Ahh," sighs Gran. "Now I see."

My voice shakes. "It's a b-big secret. I *promised* I wouldn't tell and now I have." To my surprise, I burst into tears.

Gran hugs me, forgetting her cast, and bangs me on the back.

"All right, Cassie, let's talk about this."

And we do. It seems asylum seekers can't work till they get to be called refugees and can stay in this country. Then they can work. Gran says that the government doesn't want asylum seekers to get too settled in, working and all, in case they're going to be sent back home. I find it hard to understand. Who would want to send Leyla away?

I wail to Gran, "I wish I didn't know about all this. Could they put me in jail for not telling that her brother is breaking the law?"

"Of course not," Gran says. "Let's pray now for Leyla and her family that they soon receive refugee status. Then everything will be all right."

Me, I'm shy about praying out loud with anyone listening, even Gran. I'd rather talk to God in my bedroom by myself. But Gran does the praying. And I say, "Amen."

At night I open my Diary:

Dear Diary
Saturday

But I haven't the heart to write anything.

Chapter 18

The rest of the weekend drags by. Church and Youth Group is the only time I go out. At home, Gran tries to cheer me up with games and a DVD and I pretend to be happy.

Then it's Monday and I'm not looking forward to it. More SATS practice and I keep my head down and never look Georgia's way. Leyla, the egg and I have lunch and we talk about the practice test. Then a little surprise happens. Gemma from the other class comes in late and sits down with us. I like Gemma – she's got a nice big smile and lots of freckles. I sneak a peep at her usual table and they're just finishing up. So that's the reason, but I'm chuffed anyway. She and Leyla grin at each other and Gemma shares her cake with us.

She says, "I was helping paint a poster for this Saturday's car boot sale. You'll see it by your classroom." I remember then that Gemma is an arty type.

I point out the bags of stuff stacked in the corner of the hall, and I say to Leyla, "You coming to the car boot? You could hang out with Gran and me."

"I don't know," Leyla bites her lip.

"Money from it goes for new computers and our school trip," Gemma says. "So it's a good thing to support."

Leyla is quiet for a moment. Then she says, "Maybe."

At break, when there are just the two of us, Leyla tells me, "My brother will not like the trip for me."

She gives a little sad smile. "It does not matter. We have no £50 for… um, extras."

I nod, but I know I'll not give up just yet. I plan to talk to Gran tonight.

At the end of the day, Shorty hands out leaflets – more paper aeroplanes, and I suddenly suss why they're also called flyers. More adverts, of course, about the car boot.

When I get home after school, I remind Gran about the sale. "Great!" she says. "We've got boxes of stuff to get rid of." Suddenly she waves her cast in the air and moans she can't drive yet.

We have a think and then Gran phones Mrs Barnes, our neighbour. It turns out she's got junk to unload too and is happy to fill up her big car and take us.

It's a good thing I'm a flexible kid, coz my life is just one bit of problem-solving after another. I tell Gran about Leyla not having money to go on the school trip. (Can you believe I'm worrying about Leyla when *I'm* still scraping up cash myself?)

I groan and say, "It probably doesn't matter. Her horrible brother wouldn't let her go anyway."

"Don't be too quick to judge him," Gran warns. "You don't know much about the family and their worries." She promises though to have a think about Leyla's situation.

I don't say any more, but I grit my teeth and suddenly decide it *does* matter. Every kid who wants to should go on the school trip. A little voice inside says "that includes me".

Later, I finally hear from Dad.

FROM: Dad
DATE: 23 April 21:18
TO: Cassie
SUBJECT: Still sad?

Dear Cassie,
I'm so sorry you're having a miserable time. I
couldn't answer sooner.
Two of my shipmates have been ill and I've
been doing double shifts. I just fall into my bunk
after 20 hours and can't do anything else but
work and sleep. This is my first break.
You're such a great kid that I feel sure your ex-
pals will miss you and want to be friends again.
Even with these problems, I'm glad you've made
friends with Leyla. Well done.
Give Gran my love. I'm glad she's recovering.
God bless, Dad
PS I don't worry about your tests. I remember
those ace reports you used to get in Sneezers.

Dad doesn't know. Sneezers' little school was a piece
of cake compared to SATS.

Chapter 19

Today is an ordinary Tuesday at school. No SATS practice for once. Even Shorty has been looking fed up with having to plough through the same stuff over and over. I'm "daysleeping" in class while I wonder what to take to the car boot to make school trip money. There's Mr Brown, my old teddy with one ear and one eye. I think the torn-off ear is in a drawer somewhere and the eye in a button box. Maybe Gran will sew them on. There's a lacy pink-dress horror that Gran's cousin gave me for my last birthday. Would anybody in the whole world want to wear it? Maybe the girly-girl two classes down who has hair bows and a frilly pink winter coat. In the back of my cupboard are old games and Lego to get rid of. And puzzles I'm bored with. With the extra money from Gran and some sales at the car boot, I should be getting near my trip goal! I smile and picture myself abseiling down a tower.

"Cassandra!" Shorty glares at me.

She never uses my full name. What have I done?

"I've asked you a question three times. It's no good sitting there smiling." Shorty comes to our table and stands over me. "If you are unable to answer, at least do me the courtesy of saying, 'I don't know'."

I crane up my neck to see Shorty's face and mumble, "I don't know". What I really mean is that I don't know the question!

"Thank you," Shorty says and marches back to the front.

The dinner bell rings and I'm saved further shame.

Leyla and I walk down to the hall. "You did not know the easy maths question?" she asks.

I shrug. "I'm not a maths genius like you. Anyway I was 'daysleeping'."

Leyla looks at me. "You make fun my bad English?"

"Oh, no, Leyla, I wasn't teasing. It's a lovely way to say it."

In the hall, I collect my food and Leyla opens her bag with the egg plus carrots, some dark-looking bread and juice. Gemma is back at her old table, but suddenly Lauren plonks herself down in the empty chair beside Leyla.

"Hey, Lauren," I burst out. I'm so surprised I can't think of anything to talk about. I glance over at our old table and see, even at this distance, that Georgia is fuming. Tabs tries to give her an apple, but Georgia shoves it away and it rolls on to the floor.

Finally I ask Lauren "What's with?" and nod my head to our old table.

Lauren pushes back her ginger fringe and says, "I got fed up. That's all," and she bites into her burger.

"How d'you mean?" I ask.

Lauren shrugs. "I got fed up with the same old yap, yap, blah, blah at lunch." She takes another huge mouthful of burger and chews for a while.

I wait, wondering.

Then Lauren says, "Georgia talks about nothing but you, your desertion she calls it. She thinks you're a traitor, a creep, a loser, a saddo and whatever other horrible things she can come up with. Every day it's the same."

I look over at Georgia's table and she's staring at me.

"Georgia doesn't like to lose control," I say. "She likes us all doing what she wants."

"Me, I've been looking for a way out of Georgia's clutches ever since that stupid hat thing," Lauren says. "I never wanted to wear one, but I gave in."

Leyla remembers and touches her *hijab*. It's cream-coloured today.

Lauren changes the subject. "I'm stuffed after that burger. Want my banana, Leyla?"

Leyla grins and says yes.

I glance again over at Georgia's table. She points at me and doubles over pretending to laugh. A second or two later, Tabs does the same.

"Pathetic," I say.

"Pathetic," Lauren agrees.

"What is path-e-tic?" Leyla pronounces it carefully.

"THEM!" Lauren and I cry out together. But then I explain.

Later, on my way home from school, I start feeling a little sorry for Georgia. What a wuss I am!

So Wuss Cassie texts Georgia and Tabs. And Mia, too, who wasn't in school today.

```
Silly fite. RU redy
B mates agin?
C
```

Before tea, I check for messages. There aren't any.

Chapter 20

Gran is cooking again, so for tea we have yummy casserole with jacket potatoes, and blackberry and apple tart for pudding.

I say the obvious, "You're a much better cook than me."

Gran says, "You've been a brick." She's smiling at me like that's praise. Is being a brick a good thing? She goes on, "You've been so much help shopping and cooking." She grins. "Your only *doubtful* effort was that sticky rice."

"More like bubble wrap," I say. "Or cement. Even the birds turned up their beaks," I add and we giggle.

Since there's extra pocket money for helping, Gran suggests we open my trip bank and count the dosh. (She doesn't call it "dosh".)

I cross my fingers. I'm hopeful.

"Collect your bank and I'll get the key," Gran says.

I don't know where Gran hides the key. Smart lady! But I've saved much better now that Georgia can't suck me into pea-brained buys.

Gran hands me the key and my pocket money for the week. I turn the key and reveal the treasure. At least I hope it's treasure. Seems pretty full anyway.

We stack up the coins plus the two extra fivers and count: £21.23. Result! Over half way. I do a bit of mental maths (which I'm OK at, by the way – it's mainly problems I have problems with... joke). Only £18.77 to go to make my £40 towards the trip.

Future pocket money (1) if I spend nothing (impossible) (2) minus the fivers I won't get now Gran is getting better means I'll still be some pounds short. But, there's the car boot. And… "If I weed the garden this summer, could I have the last bit ahead of time?" I ask.

Gran gives me a hug. That means yes and we lock up the money again.

I'm mega-chuffed until two things happen. I remember it's Gran's birthday next week. I used to make all my presents: sticky collages, grimy table mats and blobby clay bowls. I'm too old for that now, so some trip money will need to go for her present. Next, I check my messages.

```
U rbbish 2 like Odjb.
H8 U 4ever. G
```

My evening is spoiled and I go to bed early.

Next morning, I feel better. At least I've tried and now I can put it behind me. I'll just get on with my other friends – Leyla and now, I hope, Lauren.

A new problem strikes me. What did I say about being a flexible kid and a problem solver? Here we go again. Because, how is Leyla going to make the school trip unless I can think of something?

I get out a notebook and write:

Helping Leyla Go on the School Trip.

There are two parts to this problem. I put down:

1. Money. 2. Her brother.

Under "Money", I write:

Talk to Gran.
Ask at school.
Pray.

Under "Her brother", I don't write anything. I'll tackle that later.

At breakfast, while I munch muesli, I say to Gran, "It's so unfair that Leyla can't go on the school trip – £50 is too much for her."

Gran says, "There might be special funding to help children who can't afford to go."

"Really?" I start to smile.

Gran asks, "Would you like me to write a note to take to the head teacher?"

"Yes, please."

Forty-five minutes later, I'm standing in front of the school secretary's desk.

"Can I see Mrs Kendall? I've got a note from Gran."

The secretary knocks on the head teacher's door and gives my message. Then she turns to me, "Go on in, Cassie. Just a few minutes, mind."

Today Mrs Kendall's bright red hair is tied up in a ponytail with a green scrunchy that exactly matches her pullover. How cool is that! She smiles and takes my note. She reads it quickly and says, "Sit down a minute, Cassie, while I explain about funding for the trip."

Here's what she says. "The cost for each child is £200." (Whoah! I hadn't taken in it was so much). "Forresters Megastore sponsors £50 of that and a charity foundation another £50. We expect this Saturday's car boot profit from the entrance charge, stall, tea bar and donations, together with last Christmas' fete, to add another £50." (My head begins to swim.) Then Mrs Kendall finishes with, "That leaves each child to find £50."

I burst in, "So if the car boot makes a bit extra, could Leyla have it?" Then, I tell her about how asylum seekers don't have much money.

Mrs Kendall smiles at me again. "I'm aware of that, Cassie. I'm pleased you've made friends with Leyla and are concerned for her. But I can't give you the answer you want."

My hopes slump.

"In the two Year-6 classes, there are five asylum-seeker families. In the class for next year there are even more." Mrs Kendall shakes her head. "If we fund one child, we'll have to fund them all. As well, we would have to think of British children whose parents are short of money."

"I was just hoping for Leyla," I say. "But I understand." I trudge out of the head's office and climb the stairs to face a day of more SATS practice.

Chapter 21

After school, I pop into Patel's for a cheering Galaxy. It's not been a good day, what with Mrs Kendall's no to Leyla and two dodgy SATS. I come out tearing paper off my choc bar and see Leyla with – well it must be her brother. Not thinking, I rush up to them and gabble:

"Hello-I'm-Cassie-Leyla's-friend-at-school-and-can-she-come-with-me-and-my-Gran-to-the-car-boot-on-Saturday-it's-to-make-money-for-computers-and-our-class-school-trip-everybody's-going-and-it's-a-good-thing!" I stop for breath.

Leyla's brother glares down at me. His black moustache twitches and his fierce eyes pin me to the spot. I try, but I'm afraid to look away in case he clocks me one. When he has stared at me for an age, he turns to Leyla and speaks in harsh, crackly sounds. She answers in the same kind of words only softer. Is she telling her brother what I've said? I think so. He must not understand English as well as his sister.

But he knows one word. He suddenly steps towards me. He leans down, his black beard almost touching me, and barks, "NO!" Then, he grabs Leyla's hand and drags her into the shop.

I walk home more depressed than ever. Along with all my other mistakes, I've probably made trouble for Leyla with her family. That night I pray for her. I'm not exactly sure what to ask for so I just hope God will keep her and her family safe.

Next morning on the way into class, I say sorry to Leyla and ask if I dropped her in it.

"In what?" she says, screwing up her face.

"In trouble," I explain.

"It do not matter."

Nothing special happens that day or the next. When I come into class, Georgia bawls out, "What's that bad smell?" Most kids pretend not to hear, but Josh and Kevin smirk and snigger. They were in the hat-wearing bunch.

I ignore it. Lauren looks uncomfortable. Now I think of it, so does Tabs.

Oh yes, two something specials do happen that I should mention. Mia joins our lunch table. She's small and mousy with braces on her teeth. I can hardly believe she's got the nerve to leave Georgia's table. But her best mate is Lauren so that must explain it. Mousy or not, Mia's ace at numbers and in zero minutes she and Leyla are head-to-head. They jabber on about a tricky problem in the practice numeracy. Imagine! Yakking maths at lunch!

Then the next day, Friday lunchtime, Gemma sits with us too. She's late again coz of painting direction posters for tomorrow's car boot. We're getting to be a bunch. A new lunch bunch. I like it.

Later, I tell Gran about our growing gang. I think to myself, though, if maths is going to be the main topic, I'll have to eat somewhere else. Joke!

After tea, Gran and I drag out all the unwanted stuff for the car boot. We start packing it into the supermarket boxes Mrs Barnes has brought us.

Gran has loads of odds and ends of china from our old house in Sneezers, including *three* flowery tea sets! Dad and I never guzzled that much tea – beer and coffee for him, milk and juice for me. Where did they all come from? Gran has all white plates and bowls. She's a minimalist, she says. She has also gathered mounds of old clothes to take and some jewellery. She never wears stuff that's hideous, I'm glad to say, unlike some kids' mums. I won't mention their names. I note Gran isn't giving up the "accident boots".

My rubbish: Gran promises to fix up Mr Brown, the teddy. My Power Rangers collection goes and the lacy pink dress plus jeans and T-shirts I've grown out of. This is embarrassing – I find I've still got a Barbie doll with stacks of clothes, and Barbie's boyfriend Ken. I didn't like him much so he has only one outfit. It was all in the back of the wardrobe, honest! Also boxes of old books: mine, Gran's, and Dad's collection of sea stories.

"Are you sure we should give Dad's books away?" I ask Gran.

"I emailed him and he said get rid of the lot."

I moan, "Will the sale make any money? If everybody's junk is like ours, who will want to buy it?"

Gran laughs. "One person's junk may be another person's treasure. Some little girl will love your Barbie. You might even go shopping and find something you like."

But I don't want to spend money, I think, but don't say.

I check my emails before I go to bed and there's one from Dad.

FROM: Dad
DATE: 27 April 18:25
TO: Cassie
SUBJECT: Good luck

Dear Cassie,
Good luck for your car boot money-making tomorrow. Hope my seafaring tales sell for squillions!
Have your problems with your old friends been sorted?
I'm on watch in five minutes so must go.
Let me know about your successes tomorrow.
Love you,
Dad

Chapter 22

I wake up early coz I'm so excited. I pull the curtains and it's a sunny day. Perfect! Lots of people will come to the car boot.

Gran is up too and we eat a scrummy breakfast of bacon, fried tomatoes, scrambled egg and toast. I wash up while Gran sews on Mr Brown's ear. He's got two eyes again, too. He looks so sweet I'm almost sorry to sell him.

"I think all our things will make a good profit," says Gran, biting off the sewing cotton. "We have to pay an entrance fee of £10, which Mrs Barnes and I will share. The school *suggests* donating a percentage of sale profit to the school, but you don't have to." I remember then Mrs Kendall mentioned "donations". Gran adds, "I've promised 20 per cent. That OK with you?"

I nod – I'm really happy. Maybe I'll make the rest of my trip money. Maybe I won't have to save abso-blooming-lutely *all* my pocket money for the next month. Mrs Barnes helps us take our stuff to her car. Gran can still only carry with one arm, but her ankle is fine now. We go through the school gate into the car park promptly at 9.30. The buyers come in at 10, hope, hope.

We take a folding table out of the back of the car and I make a display of the Power Rangers, Barbie and Ken, Mr Brown and the games and books. I'm too ashamed to have the pink dress with my stuff, but Mrs Barnes has brought a rail to hang things, so that's OK.

I take my black pen and sticky labels and scribble on prices.

25p   £1   £5   50p
Everything on this tray — 10p

Ten o'clock comes and in pour masses of people. And Leyla!

"Hey, Leyla. I didn't know you could come!" I cry.

"I explain to Mama that today is for school. To buy things for school," Leyla gives a big grin. "Mama is strong for, ah, ed-cation. Is that right, Cassie?"

"Ed-u-cation," I say and to my surprise I give Leyla a big hug, half knocking off her headscarf.

She pulls it back into place and says, "I do not have things to sell."

"Never mind. You can help me," I say.

People look at our stuff and walk on. I begin to lose hope. Then a little girl with blue bows in her hair and shiny patent leather shoes stares and stares at Barbie. Her mum rifles through the clothes on the rail.

I hope for £5 for Barbie and clothes. (I'll probably have to *give* Ken away. Who'd want him?) The little girl opens her hand and I see three gold coins – £3.

"Can I buy Barbie?" she says.

"Well—" I'm thinking...

Then her mum comes over with the pink dress and says, "Isn't this lovely, darling? It's too big now, but by next year..." and she holds the horror up against the little girl.

I feel so sorry for the kid that I let her buy Barbie for £3.

Meanwhile Leyla has sold two of my books and a game. Mr Brown has gone too. I'm sorry I didn't say goodbye. And suddenly there's a big rush of kids and grown-ups and all of us, Gran and Mrs Barnes too, sell lots of things.

Then there's a bit of a lull. Gran says, "Why don't you two go and have a look round?" And she gives Leyla and me each £2. Leyla tries hard not to take it, but Gran insists. I see Georgia and Tabs round a 4x4 near the entrance, so we go the other way.

"Maybe I'll find a birthday present for Gran," I say to Leyla. "It's next week."

I've got a little pocket money to put with the £2.

We drift round, peering here and there, picking up things and putting them back. We don't see anything we want. Finally, we come to a big white van with loads of stuff mixed up in boxes, with different prices on each box. I don't see anything very interesting.

Then Leyla shows me a £1 box with odds and ends of china.

"Maybe a birthday present in there?" she suggests.

I paw through it and spot a white cup with ripply edges and then I see, under an old rusty tin tea caddy, its saucer. Yes – a match! They would look nice on Gran's kitchen shelf and they're all white like she likes. I buy the box and think maybe we can sell the other bits at our car.

"Shall I buy these plates?" asks Leyla. Taped together are three smart green and blue plates and three mugs for £1.50. "We do not have any dishes like, um…?"

"Matching?" I offer.

"Yes! Matching!" she says, pleased.

"Go for it," I say, and she does.

We stroll back to our car. While Gran and Mrs Barnes go for tea, I slip out the cup and saucer. I roll bubble wrap round the two pieces and stow them in the back seat.

Leyla and I sort through my box. I twist hard on the tea caddy's rusty lid, but it won't come off. The caddy's heavy so there's something inside.

Chapter 23

Leyla has a try at the caddy lid, but has no success either. "You need a—" and she makes a picture in the air with her hands.

I don't understand. "Do it again." She does, doing twisting motions towards the caddy.

"A screwdriver!" I cry.

"Yes!" she shouts. First time Leyla's been *loud*.

I scrabble through the back of Mrs B's car, looking for a toolbox. There's a grey bag with a string tie and inside, yes, a screwdriver.

Leyla holds the caddy still and I prod and stab at the lid. Finally, with a shower of rust, it comes off.

Inside is newspaper. It's wrapped round something.

Leyla and I bend over the something while I peel off the paper. You'd think we were expecting to find gold.

What we do find is a pointed little piece of china. I'm so disappointed, but whatever was I hoping for? It's pretty though, a little cottage scene on the four sides and a few holes on the top.

"Oh well," I say to Leyla, "I can probably sell it for a pound. And that was the price of the whole box."

I pick up the piece again and turn it all round. It reminds me of something but I can't think what.

A couple of gel-haired boys turn up and open the game boxes I have left. It takes ten minutes for them to choose one for 15p. Meanwhile, something about the pointy piece niggles at the back of my mind. Maybe it's because I could make it another bit of

Gran's birthday present. She might like it even though it's not all white.

I keep on thinking about the piece while Leyla sells a dress and two tops to a woman wearing a *hijab* headscarf like Leyla. They talk English though, so she can't be from Leyla's country.

Suddenly, I've got it. I know where I've seen something like the pointy piece. I'm so bursting with hope I can't wait for Gran to come back from tea.

And here she comes, with ice cream cornets for Leyla and me.

"Gran," I cry, "I've got, um, um, *something* to s-show you." I stammer, I'm so excited.

"Eat your ice creams first," says Gran. "Look, they're starting to drip."

I wolf down my cornet so fast it makes my forehead hurt. Then, I say, "Gran, what about this?" and I hold out the pointy china piece. "I bought it in a box of mixed stuff and it's like… like something I saw in a magazine in your shop!"

Gran looks stunned. Her mouth falls open. She takes the piece, turns it round and round and upside down, then stares at me. Her eyes are very wide.

"Cassie, I don't believe it. What you've got here is a piece by Clarice Cliff!" She points to the name on the bottom.

Leyla takes my hand and we say together, "Who's that?"

"Clarice Cliff is a very famous ceramic designer who worked in the early twentieth century. Her best designs go for hundreds of pounds. Especially ones like this."

"Hundreds of pounds!" I shout. People goggle at me from the cars on both sides of us.

Gran gives me a hug and says, "Ssshh."

"Can people really pay hundreds for a little china pointy thing?" I'm hoping it's true, but it's hard to take in.

"They can and do," says Gran. She rotates the thing again slowly. "It's a sugar sifter and it's beautifully painted. I'm absolutely certain it's genuine."

"Sugar sifter," I say to myself. Doesn't sound very useful, but who cares?

Gran says, "The first thing to do is find the people who sold it to you. They can't have known what it was." She glances at me, "We must share the value with them. Don't you agree, Cassie?"

I bite my lip. "But I *bought* it! It was in *there*." I snatch up the old tea caddy and tell her the trouble Leyla and I had getting it open.

Gran says, "They might be poor and this will be wonderful for them too."

I'm grudging, but I say OK. "It's the big white van over there, next to the red car with stickers." But there's a space next to the red car. "They've gone!"

Mrs Barnes, who has just come back, says she'll hold the fort and Gran, Leyla and I hurry over to the red car. Gran asks a man wearing an Arsenal T-shirt if he knows the people in the white van.

"Nah!" he answers. "They're traders. They said they were off to a better car boot."

"Did you notice their number plate?" asks Gran.

"Nah, sorry," says Arsenal T-shirt.

"Oh," says Gran. "Thanks anyway."

The people on the other side of the space don't know them or their number plate either.

On the outside, I say, "Well, we tried." On the inside, I think, Yessssss!

But Gran's not done looking. "We'll ask the school organisers," she says. "The traders probably booked a space ahead, paying and giving name and number plate."

Nooooooooooooooooooooo! Gran is so determined to give our money away!

Chapter 24

Mrs Barnes minds our car boot stall again while Gran, Leyla and I head on inside the school.

TEA BAR INFORMATION

My heart clunks down to my trainers when I see it's Shorty on the Information desk. She's bound to search high and low for the van traders.

Gran tells Shorty the news about our find. Then she gives the space number of the van, which she got from the red car people. Shorty scans down her clipboard list. Then she does it again, and again. I clutch Leyla's hand.

Shorty looks up. (That makes a first – normally she looks *down*.) "No, sorry, that space wasn't booked ahead. The people came in today and paid at the entrance."

Wow! We've done the right thing, I guess, and still the pointy job is ours! Gran agrees we can stop looking.

We troop back to Mrs B and I begin to think what to do with my treasure. When I say "treasure" to myself, I remember Gran saying, "One person's junk is another's treasure." She wasn't wrong!

Gran gets on her mobile to her boss at the ceramic gallery to check on price. Leyla and I lean near to listen. Gran says into her mobile, "You estimate £250 to £300 at auction, with a reserve of £225? That right?"

Leyla and I hug each other.

"Right," I say to Leyla. "That's the rest of my school trip paid for. And your trip too. And money for school computers."

"My trip?" says Leyla, her face one big fat question mark.

"You helped me find it," I remind her.

"Cassie, you are so, so…" Leyla stops, shutting her eyes to think of the word she wants.

"Wonderful?" I offer.

"Yes," she laughs. And then, "Generous, I meant too. But I do not think my brother let me go."

Just then, people start to roll up and ask to see the sugar sifter. Shorty told Mrs Kendall, the head. Mrs Kendall told the tea bar staff, and the tea bar staff told their kids. And pretty soon everybody has heard about my £1 treasure. The red car people come and those on the other side of the van. And Josh and Kevin, Mia and Lauren and Gemma and Guler, and two more Kurdish girls from the other class. And, naturally, Mrs Kendall herself.

While all these people are crowding round, I notice Mrs Barnes quietly goes on selling almost all the rest of our stuff.

The next thing I notice is Georgia and Tabs at the edge of the crowd. I watch as they work their way through to Gran, still holding the pointy piece.

"That looks a right bit of rubbish, doesn't it, Tabs?" Georgia raises her voice so everybody around can hear. "I wouldn't pay 10p for it."

Gran says quietly, "It's a good thing, then, that we weren't planning to sell it to you!" She smiles at Georgia, even though she knows how Georgia has treated me. Explaining, she says, "Clarice Cliff china is bought by collectors all over the country."

Tabs pipes up, "I think it's pretty. I love the little cottage."

Georgia gives her a furious look and pinches her arm.

"Ow! Stop it!" cries Tabs and pushes Georgia away. Georgia tumbles backwards – as I said before, Tabs never knows her own strength. Georgia crashes down on a tall man's feet.

He scoops her up off his shoes and asks, "You all right, little girl?"

Georgia rudely swats his arm away and marches off, her nose in the air.

Tabs stares after her and heaves a big sigh. "Georgia is well boring these days. She's a complete grump since you left."

"Come and be with us," I say.

Our car hardly has anything left to sell, so Tabs, Leyla and I drift round and I buy us all lemonades with the rest of Gran's money. We sit on a bench to drink them.

Suddenly, Leyla says, "What time is it?" She doesn't have a watch.

"Four thirty," I say.

"Oh, I must go now. I told Mama I am back by then."

Here's my chance. "I'll go with you and help explain," I say.

"No, no, my brother…"

But I insist, saying we have good news to tell her. We say goodbye to Tabs and tell Gran where we're going. I whisper in Gran's ear my hopes and I promise to be home by six o'clock or earlier.

As we hurry out of the school gate, I pray her brother isn't home. I remember his fierce eyes, black beard and twitching moustache and I shiver.

Chapter 25

Leyla's home is very near the supermarket. It's a terraced brick house with four flats and Leyla's flat is upstairs. The entrance round the side is crowded with a pushchair and a battered old bike.

"The other top flat has a baby. The bike is my brother's," says Leyla.

I shiver again. That must mean he's at home. I had hoped he was at work.

We go in. Her mum is resting on a sofa with her feet up. She is small and thin like Leyla with tired-looking brown eyes with dark circles. Her hair is almost grey and pulled back in a bun. She doesn't have a scarf and I remember Leyla saying they don't wear a *hijab* at home.

"This is Cassie, my friend from school," says Leyla, pulling off her blue scarf.

For the first time, I see her shiny, long brown hair.

Her mum smiles and holds out her hand. I take it and say hello. Her mum speaks with the sharp, crackly sounds I heard before.

Leyla translates. "Mama says, please sit. She knows you are a kind girl."

I feel my face go hot and mumble, "Thank you." I look round the small room and towards the even tinier kitchen. But I don't see the brother. I begin to relax and plonk down on a wooden chair.

"Will you tell your mum about the sugar sifter? Don't forget to say you helped me find it so it's fair for you to get money for the school trip."

Leyla begins to talk. Her eyes are bright and her hands move fast, showing the shape of the sugar sifter. I hear the word "pounds" in the middle.

Leyla's mum clasps her face in surprise. I think she must be asking, "How can this be?"

Suddenly I hear quick, thumping feet on the stairs. The door bursts open and there's her brother!

He seems to fill the room. He speaks loud and fast. I can hear it's a question.

I shrivel in my chair. I know he's wondering what I'm doing here.

Leyla's mum says something stern and points to another chair like mine. The brother makes a disgusted snort and sits down.

Leyla says to me, "Mama says our people are famous for welcome to visitors. And he should welcome too." Then she says, "This is my brother Hassan, Cassie." She turns to her brother and her sentence ends in "Cassie".

With a grumpy face, Hassan says, "Hello."

I say, "Hello, Hassan."

We sit in silence for a moment. Then I take a deep breath and say to Leyla, "Tell your mum that the school trip is for ed-u-cation. We will learn about the plants and animals and birds and rocks where the camp is."

Leyla speaks to her mum who, I think, looks interested.

I try to dredge up what else. My mate Chloe from last year's Year 6 told me all the good stuff from the trip. But I don't want to scare Leyla's mum. So, no use describing the assault course or abseiling or go-karting. Nor coming down in a harness from a tree platform 15 metres up. Another no-no, canoe capsize drill in a pool. Pool! That's it.

"Leyla will be able to learn to swim," I say.

She translates this. Her brother springs out of his chair and shouts something.

Leyla says, "My brother says I cannot swim with boys."

"No," I say, "the boys do something else while the girls swim." I hope this is true.

Hassan sits back down.

My brain scrabbles for something else ed-u-cational. "We can learn craft stuff, like weaving a basket." Though what saddo would choose that over abseiling?

I can see Leyla's mum likes the basket idea. Am I winning? I hope so. "It is only for a week and we learn so much," I say, looking directly at Leyla's mum. I use the word "learn" every time I can.

More quick, excited-sounding talk goes on while I wait.

"Mama says I have clothes only for school and the mosque," Leyla explains.

"No problem. The sugar sifter money will easily run to trousers, some T-shirts and a swimsuit. For swimming with the girls," I say carefully.

Suddenly Leyla's brother jumps up from his chair and speaks fast, nearly shouting, and waving his arms. In the middle of this he points at me. Finally he runs out of breath and stops.

A very calm reply comes from Leyla's mum, which takes some time. Leyla and I both wait. Then Leyla's brother stomps out of the room and back down the stairs.

I'm getting really stressed when, at *last*, Leyla's mum looks at me and says one word.

Chapter 26

Leyla spins round and her long hair goes flying. "Oh, Cassie," she cries. "Mama says YES!"

I grab her hand and we dance round and round, hugging each other.

When we stop, breathless, Leyla's mum smiles at me, and says, according to Leyla, that I am a good friend. I am! I am! I think so too.

Leyla translates some more, "Mama says I am allowed school things and learning things." She giggles. "Mama says it nicer than I can make in English."

"You make English just fine!" I say.

"Mama asks, also, you forgive Hassan, um, being rude. She says he has to be man of the family and it is heavy for him."

"Do you mean a burden?"

"A burden, I think so."

I understand, sort of. Being a flexible kid with Dad far away is a burden for me sometimes too.

Leyla's mum gives Leyla what seems like instructions and Leyla goes into the kitchen. She comes back soon with tea in a glass and no milk and tiny little crispy biscuits.

"This is how we drink tea in our country," says Leyla.

It's very hot without any cooling milk and I burn my tongue. But I like it. Sweet and a little bit spicy and the bikkies are lovely.

All at once I look at my watch. I realise I'll have to shift to get home when I promised. I shake hands with Leyla's mum and thank her.

Then I scorch up the road, completely and abso-blooming-lutely happy.

I sprint in the door in time, just, and tell Gran the great news. Then I go to email Dad.

FROM: Cassie
DATE: 28 April 18:30
TO: Dad
SUBJECT: TREASURE!!!!!

Dear Dad,
You won't believe it!!!!! At the car boot sale, I bought a £1 box of mixed stuff and in an old, rusty tea caddy was a Clarice Cliff china sugar sifter. You probably haven't heard of her, but Gran and her boss say it's worth loads of money, maybe up to £300. I make that £299 profit. Like, mega-amazing! So both Leyla and I are sorted for school trip money and even gear to wear. Leyla's brother got in a right mood, but her mum said she could go. Yay! Yay! Yay! A million times.
Love, Cassie
PS Also I made £14 on my car boot stuff!
Nobody bought Barbie's Ken.

Dad was on his laptop and answered straightaway.

FROM: Dad
DATE: 28 April 20:40
TO: Cassie

SUBJECT: Mega congratulations!!!! More good news!!!!!

Terrific news! I'm delighted to hear about your find – what a clever clogs to recognise you'd got something special! I'm pleased as well because Gran tells me you've worked and saved a lot for your trip and now can share your "treasure" with Leyla and the school. More good news! The powers that be have decided my ship needs a refit. So we'll be into port in the UK much earlier than expected. It'll be about the last week in July and I'll have six weeks leave. Should coincide nicely with your school holidays.
See you soon, love.
God bless, Dad
PS Poor Ken.

I run to tell Gran and we grab each other and dance round like I did with Leyla. Everything I wanted and hoped for has happened all in one day. I count my blessings, as Dad says to do.

My school trip money sorted
Dad's coming home sooner than we thought
Leyla allowed to go on school trip
Leyla's school trip money sorted
Money for Gran's birthday present
Sporty gear money for Leyla and me
Tabs a friend again

That's the main ones, but I could add me braving Leyla's brother. And making friends with Leyla's mum. Georgia falling down and huffing off crosses my mind, but I don't include it. Bad luck for somebody, even Georgia, doesn't count as a blessing.

As I take off my clothes and pull on my big T-shirt for bed, I tell God all about everything. I know he knows already, but I think he likes to hear how I feel about it. I put lots of thanks in coz I think it's easy to ask for things and not remember to be grateful afterwards. And, wow, am I grateful! I jump up and trampoline on my bed like I used to do as a little kid. It's the end of the most brilliant day there's ever been!

Last Word – I Promise

I thought my story was done, but then I was thinking I'd mention how it all turned out. I've just been typing an email to Dad.

FROM: Cassie
DATE: 18 July 18:30
TO: Dad
SUBJECT: Fantastic news!

Dear Dad,
Thanks for your phone call. Glad you got your laptop fixed. At last!!!! I really missed our emails. Gran says we can come down to the port to meet your ship on Friday. Yay!!! Only a half day of school left. Yay, again! Shorty has been tired of lessons for at least two weeks. Did OK on my SATS (Shorty surprised—me too!). Can you believe my junior school "career" is over? The last six weeks have whizzed by with the school trip and parties and stuff. You know that Gran loaned me money ahead for Leyla's trip and mine till the sugar sifter was sold. Anyway, it didn't go to auction after all. Instead, a collector bought it direct for £350! Isn't that super-trillion-amazing????
I gave Gran a beautiful honey-coloured pullover for a late birthday present and the school computers got money too.
Will tell you more about SATS "triumph" and all about the school trip when you're here. Can't wait!!!!!
Love, Cassie

Dad will crack up to hear about all the fun and funny things that happened on the trip. Even more activities than I knew about before from Chloe – like tunnelling in special sunk drainpipes, a rope bridge, a canoe river trip, raft building (ours fell apart), crabbing, a walk on the beach, learning about rock pools, and quizzes about local birds and animals. (These last things impressed Leyla's mum when she got home.) Leyla also made a basket for her mum (while I went canoeing).

Leyla turned out mega-sporty. I've decided she's a flexible kid too. We asked for a special girls' swim and she managed to float right away. She wore her *hijab* the whole time (except when she wore a cap in the pool) but pinned with about twenty hairgrips so it wouldn't fall off when we did abseiling and all that. I did frizbee and rounders but I wasn't into playing football. Leyla was though, along with two other girls. Leyla scored two goals so now she's got respect. No Oddjob names any more.

It helped that Georgia didn't go on the trip. At the last minute, she strutted round telling everyone, "I'm not going on any boring old kiddy school trip. Jasper and Hortensia are taking me to Barbados. I'll be tanning deliciously in the sun and chatting up gorge boys while you lot are stuck with sweaty sports."

Georgia's not going to our secondary school in the autumn – she's off to a boarding school in the West Country. The class is over the moon at the thought of not having to listen to her any more. Sometimes I almost feel sorry for her. Almost.

Dear Diary
Wednesday
Now there's something I can't reveal,
even to Dad or Gran so, Diary, you'll
have to keep my secret. Leyla told me
her dad is in the bunch working
against Kryz's bad government. They
were hunting for him and threatened
the family if he didn't give himself up.
Instead, her mum, Hassan and Leyla
ran away through Turkey, stayed there
a year, then came on here.

The family keep what Gran calls a
low profile, using her mum's maiden
name, coz their government has an
office in London. So it wasn't only
about Hassan's job that worried Leyla.
I had to promise, promise, promise
never to tell any of this, so I never will.
Not till the good bunch wins and Leyla
can go home. She says when that
happens, not if.

Well, that's it. Everything's turned
out really GREAT. And sorry, Diary, but
this is goodbye. I won't have time to

write at secondary school - be too busy
studying. Joke. (I hope!)